"The Legends of Rasa is dreamy, glittery, and soft, reminiscent of the stories I loved as a child. An absolute must-have for fans of HTTYD and Ghibli!"

—BETHANY MEYER

(Author of *Robbing Centaurs and Other Bad Ideas*)

"Effie Joe Stock has draws you into a world of magic with these tales, each one full of characters you'll fall quickly in love with! Even if you've never stepped foot in Rasa, this short story collection will make you feel like you're home."

—KATE KORSAK

(Author of *Guardian*)

THE LEGENDS OF RASA

VOLUME I

EFFIE JOE STOCK

Third Installment in the Rasaverse

Legends of Rasa (Volume I):
A Cozy, Slice-of-Life Fantasy Story Collection

Paperback ISBN: 978-1-962337-03-8
Hardback ISBN: 978-1-962337-04-5

Published in Hackett, AR, USA by Dragon Bone Publishing™ 2024.

Cover design and illustrations are created by and copyright of Effie Joe Stock.

Interior formatting by Effie Joe Stock

Dedicated to all the side characters and worldbuilding with such intricate backstories and importance but not nearly enough page time.

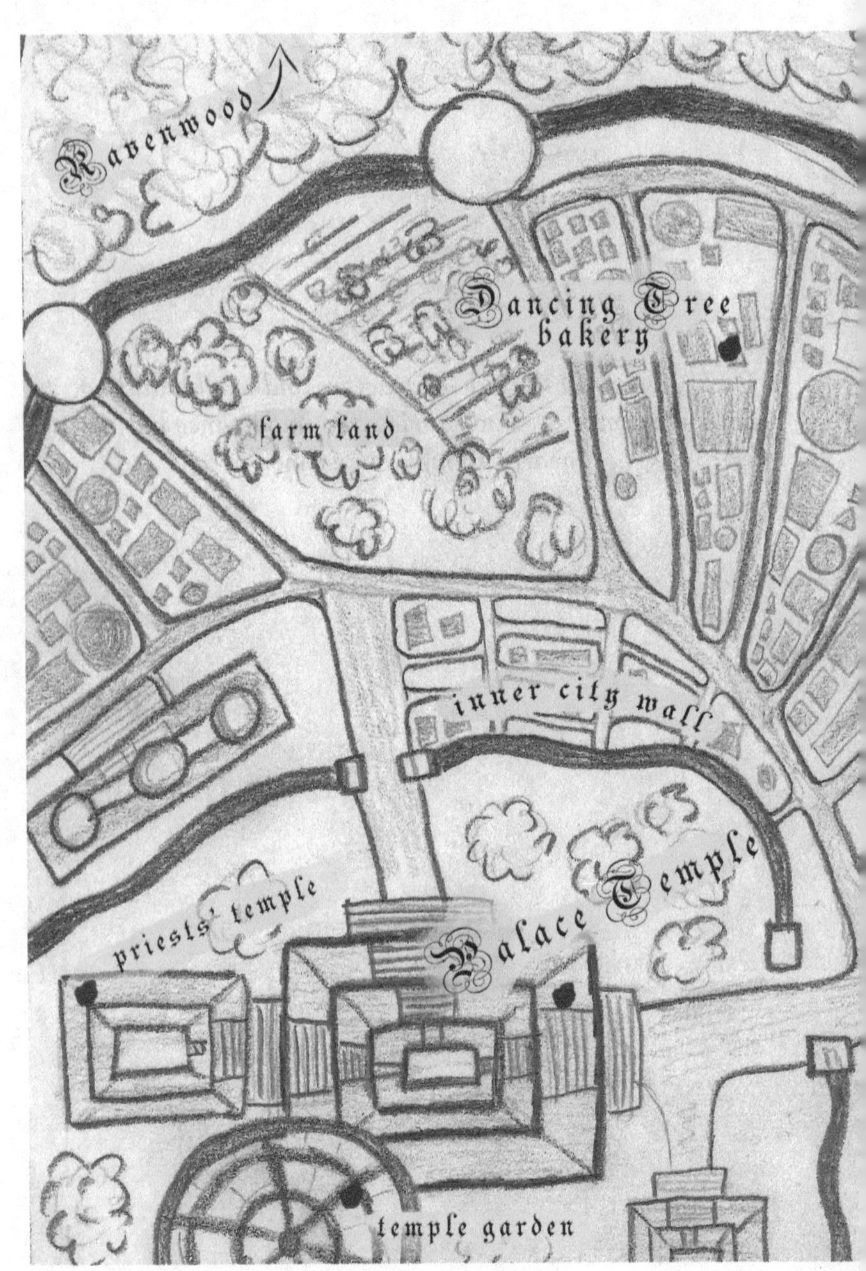
Ravenwood
Dancing Tree bakery
farm land
inner city wall
priests' temple
Palace Temple
temple garden

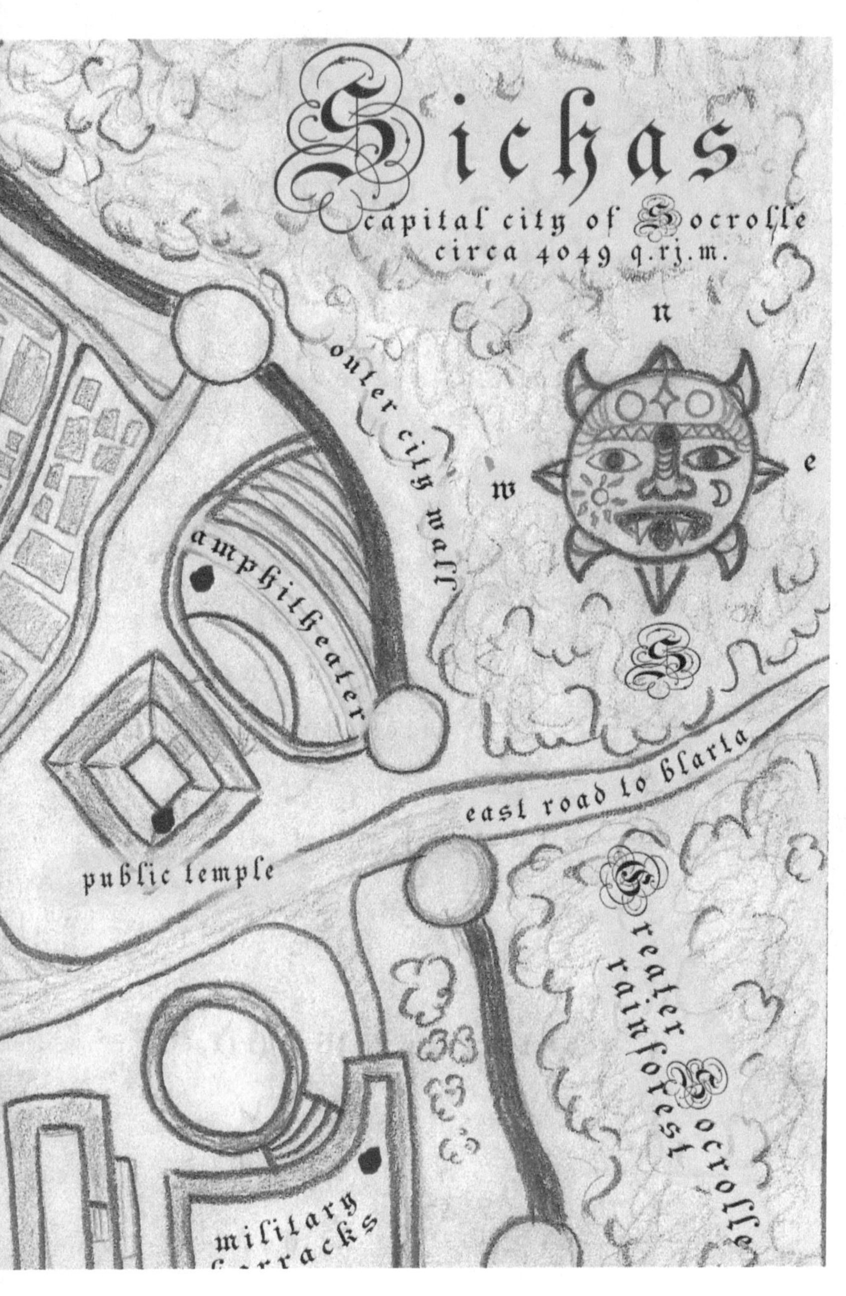
Sichas
capital city of Socrolle
circa 4049 q.rj.m.
n
w
e
outer city wall
amphitheater
east road to blarta
public temple
greater socrolle rainforest
military barracks

Duvarharia
Dragon Palace
Suźesrusum
Yazkuza
Hatching Grounds
Trans-Fall
N
Ravenwood
Socrolle

Ventronovia
Cavos Desert
Nor
New-Fars
Human Domain
Odessa

PLAYLIST

A VERY HUNGRY MUSE

"Pure as the Driven Snow" (From "The Ballad of Songbirds and Snakes") — Rachel Zegler, The Covey Band

"Itusano Island" — Mel Matthews

"Vokul Fen Mah" — Malukah

"Leaving the Shire" — Nicostrauss

"Outlander" (The Skyeboat Song) — Bear McCreary, Raya Yarbrough

"Hug Air A' Bhonaid Mhoir" — Julie Fowlis

"Into the Open Air" (From "Brave" Soundtrack) — Julie Fowlis

"Dancing in the Tavern" — Tartalo Music

SILENCE OF SLEEP IN A FOREST SO DEEP

"The Nine Walkers" — Nicostrauss

"Healing Chant" — Heather Alexander

"The Shadow Over Mirkwood" — Nicostrauss

"Dämmertal" — Elane

"Romantic Flight" — John Powell

DREAMING OF FREEDOM AND PASTRIES

"Noble Maiden Fair" (From "Brave" Soundtrack) — Emma Thompson, Peigi Baker

"Touch the Sky" (From "Brave" Soundtrack) — Julie Fowlis

"Test Flight" — John Powell

"Las Alturas" (High Places) — Liona Boyd

"The Gray Pilgrim" — Nicostrauss

"This Wish" — Ariana DeBose, Disney

A MATCHMAKING MEDIC

"Leafmen" — Danny Elfman, Pete Anthony

"The Games" (From "Brave" Soundtrack) — Patrick Doyle

"Resurrection" —Nicostrauss

"New Tail" — John Powell

"Comin' Thro' the Rye" — Bear McCreary

"Amas Veritas" — Alan Silvestri

GROUNDED TOGETHER

"The Selection" — Danny Elfman, Pete Anthony

"Moonhaven Parade" — Danny Elfman, Pete Anthony

"Aragorn the Dunedain" — Nicostrauss

"Overture and A Prisoner of the Crusades" — Micheal Kamen

"Tara's Gift" — Danny Elfman, Pete Anthony

"Party in the Shire" — Chance Thomas

"Fate Has Smiled Upon Us" — Marc Streitenfeld

"Keltiar Lands" — Tartalo Music

LISTEN TO THE COMPLETE PLAYLIST ON SPOTIFY:

The Legends of Rasa Vol. I by Effie Joe Stock

A Cozy Slice-of-Life Fantasy Story Collection

THE LEGENDS OF RASA
VOLUME I

EFFIE JOE STOCK

A VERY HUNGRY MUSE

Dragon Palace Valley, Duvarharia
Year: Rumi 1532 Q.RJ.M

"NOW WHERE DID I PUT that new crate of jerky?" Krasomila peered into the back of the dark cupboard. The hardwood floors dug into her knees as she leaned in farther. She could've sworn she'd ordered an extra case of *rusadabe* jerky just last week.

Deciding to check her records once more, she started backing out of the cabinet. *Crack!* With a passionate curse, Krasomila clutched the top of her head and staggered to her feet. The thick oak cupboards were unyielding, and a lump would stand proud on the top of her head by tomorrow.

Thinking back to the countless hours she'd spent at magic academy, drilled endlessly on different spells, magic types, intentions, and concentration, she muttered a simple healing spell.

A spark of purple magic jumped from her hand to her head. The forming bruise tingled, but the pain hardly lessened.

"Maybe, if you'd spent more time actually paying attention in class rather than writing song lyrics, you wouldn't have to suffer the horrible headache I'm sure you're going to have."

Krasomila rolled her eyes at the familiar voice. "Thank you for reminding me of that, Metej." Her words were sharper than she intended, but as always, Metej remained unfazed. Tying off the end of a waist-long, baby blue braid, he flipped the length of hair over his shoulder, absently pulling out a few strands to frame his face. He'd been doing that since they met at the academy almost seven years ago; his attention to fashion never ceased to put a small smile on Krasomila's face. "Come for your usual?" She picked her rag off the cupboard and shut its doors, promising to find the missing *rusadabe* jerky later.

"Actually"—his body language shifted from its usual nonchalant demeanor—"I was coming to check on you."

The smile on Krasomila's face faltered. "Oh." Words jumbled in her mouth as she moved past him. She felt his eyes on her as they made their way out of the back storage into the tavern's main room. She took her post behind the bar and he on one of the stools near the register—as they always did. "Why would you? I'm perfectly fine." She was aware of how perfectly *not fine* her words sounded.

His sly smile returned as he spun a coin on the polished wood bar top. When he caught the coin, it rang against the rings decorating every one of his fingers. "You haven't sung in nearly a month. Usually, you have a new sheet of lyrics or poetry you want me to look over every week. And your lyre's hook has been rather empty." He nodded to where her lyre usually hung on the wall.

A blush burned her cheeks.

"I just thought maybe ...?"

Krasomila wiped her mouth and laughed, the hollow sound echoing in the empty tavern. She ducked under the bar to hide the uncertainty on her face, which matched the flipping in her stomach. Grabbing a full bottle of *lurujmu fuju*, she moved it to the shelves behind her, replacing the nearly empty bottle. Setting it before him, she nodded. "Drink the rest. It's on the house."

"Krasomila," his pale hand paused on hers, the tattoos on his forearm mingling perfectly with his shining yellow Shalnoa. "Why won't you tell me what's wrong? Are you in trouble? Is it your family?"

Knowing she couldn't escape his persistence and surprised he'd waited even this long to bring it up, she swallowed around the lump in her throat, eyes never leaving their touching hands "No ... they haven't bothered me since ..." Her teeth tugged at her lips as she shoved down years of unwanted memories. "I haven't seen them for a long time. I just—" She shook her head. Sharing her problems had never come easy to her, and even after knowing Metej for seven years, she still found it difficult to open to him. Listening to hundreds of strangers pour out their problems on her while she worked hard to run the tavern every night had all but annihilated her appetite for sharing emotions.

His eyes flitted between her eyes and their hands; after a heavy sigh, he withdrew from the contact. Swiping a shot glass from the other side of the bar, he poured himself a drink and threw it back. The way he easily downed shots of *lurujmu fuju* never ceased to impress her nor bring back memories of when they met—he'd been the first and only Duvarharian to best her in a drinking competition.

"Do you remember that day?"

Though she snapped back from the memory, nostalgic, wild excitement still riveted in her veins. Shaking her head, she fell to wiping the counter, even though it was already immaculate. "How could I forget?"

"After fifteen shots of *lurujmu fuju*, any sane Duvarharian would forget."

"I'm not sane."

"I know." He winked then downed another shot before pouring a third. This time, he pushed it to her. "Indulge me, Kras."

The old nickname elicited a blush on her cheeks. "Don't call me that."

"Why not?"

"Because—"

"Because it brings back memories of us?"

Krasomila paused her cleaning, struggling against wanting to forget and wanting to live the memories all over again: late nights sneaking out of the academy and into the *Suźefrusum* forest, swimming bare under the moons' light in the Itona lake with Aqua Dragons, and playing music together—an accordion in his hands, a lyre in hers, and their voices mingling in harmony. But those days also reminded her of the life she'd suffered: being disowned by her parents, nights spent scouring the Dragon Palace's scraps for food, blood staining her hands when she finally found a way to make money. With a deep breath, she buried all the memories, including the good ones, because they inevitably brought the darkness with them. Her tavern opened because she'd wanted, *needed*, a new life. Nothing could compromise that; she wouldn't let it. She shrugged. "That was a different time. I was different back then."

An unconvinced look crossed his face, but he didn't press her. Instead, he nodded to the shot glass. "It's on me."

"It's already on the house," she grumbled but took the shot anyway. The smooth liquid burned on the way down, but the sweet, nutty aftertaste, mixed with the charred oak barrels the drink aged in, left a warm feeling in her soul. With a deep sigh, she pushed the glass back and watched as he downed his third shot. Already, his cheeks were rosy and his eyes sparkling, but unlike many of her other patrons, Metej didn't grow loud or rowdy; instead, the *lurujmu fuju's* influence made him more sensitive and philosophical, taking the edge off his sarcasm and dry humor.

"It's not going to work." Her eyes narrowed, but he only shrugged, propping his elbows on the bar.

"I haven't the slightest idea what you're going on about." But the twinkle in his eyes told her he knew *exactly* what she was 'going on about'.

"Fine." She tossed the rag to the other end of the bar so she'd stop fiddling with it. "I'm losing money. Fast. Faster than oiled dragon scales."

Though he chuckled, concern weighed down his voice as he swirled the *lurujmu fuju* bottle; the last of the golden drink caught the warmth of the tavern's lanterns. "But the tavern is full every night. You can hardly keep up with them, even with the new staff."

Sagging against the counter, she flicked at the gold bangles around his wrists; they matched the rings in his light blue hair. He'd always dressed better, richer, than her; it had a lot to do with their backgrounds. But that made her even more confused as to why he'd been so enamored with her. In her opinion, nothing about her screamed desirable: dirty layered skirts, tangled black curls that more often turned into an afro, average fingers she never let grow proper nails because she abhorred impracticality. "I know, and yet I'm not making anything back. My savings is nearly gone, and each week, I struggle a little more to find money up-front to restock. Then when I think I have my records straight, I keep coming up short on shipments. Just today, I've lost an entire case of *rusadabe* jerky."

His gaze darkened as he gripped the bottle tighter. The scar on his left cheek twitched—something she knew happened when he was angry. The twitch had never been triggered by her, not even when she spilled drinks on his expensive silk shirts or lost jewelry he'd gifted her. After seeing him smash another rider's face into a bar years ago after the offender groped one of the servers, she'd vowed never to get on the wrong side of his anger.

"Are you being robbed?"

Krasomila wanted to shake her head and say 'no', but she couldn't be sure. The only other explanation would be ineptitude with the accounts and coins. A lump rose into her throat. He must've noticed her lip quiver because he placed his hand over hers again, their opposite skin tones complimenting each other. "You're not a bad accountant or manager, so don't even start with that *xeneluch ue*."

Grumbling, she rolled her eyes. He knew her too well. "I'm not, but"—she wagged a finger in his face before he could interrupt—"what else could it be? I lock the doors every night. I use the protection spells I learned from the academy. And every morning I come back, the doors are still locked, the windows in one piece, and the wards in place." If she'd learned one thing from the academy, it was protection wards.

He knew that more than anyone.

"But then that'd mean you're bad with money." He scoffed, placing the bottle's rim to his lips before he paused. "And we both know that's not true." The last of the *lurujmu fuju* slipped between his lips. She stared wistfully after it, regretting letting him have the rest.

"I don't know what else it could be."

Standing, he stretched, the hem of his shirt rising just past his belt, exposing his silvery pale skin. When he caught her staring, she couldn't do anything to hide her embarrassment.

"You know ..." His voice was soft as he reached out a hand, hovering it just over the messy curls by her ear. He used to braid her hair, taming it into tight rows against her head and down her back, decorating them with beads and rings. No one had touched her hair for years, sometimes not even herself. She resisted leaning into his touch. "You haven't changed all that much. Neither of us has, I think."

He was right, but the thought of opening her heart and soul right now felt as painful as the potentiality of losing the tavern. This was her home, her dream at stake, and if she failed, if she lost this …

"Maybe not, but I can't go through that again."

"It wasn't me."

"But it *was* me."

A small, sad smile lifted the corners of his lips as he drew away. "I'll cast some detection wards around the building and the stock. If anyone tries to take something, I'll know, and I'll stop them." The fire in his icy eyes told her he would do more than stop them. "And if you need money …"

Taking a step back from the bar, from him, she shook her head. "No. You know I don't want that. Not from you."

"I know. But I'll always offer."

She clenched her jaw and fists and tried to remind herself the demons in her rearing their ugly heads were not directed against him; his wasn't the blood of vengeance they thirsted for. Taking a deep breath, she let go of the violence that had once lived in her veins. Protecting her dream by accepting Metej's help was worth a damaged ego.

"Thank you, Metej. You know you don't have to do this."

His eyebrows raised, but he only shrugged. "You know me." She did—more than anyone else, more than herself. "I don't *have* to do anything."

With one last nod, he turned and strode out of the tavern, having to duck under the low doorway. When the door closed behind him, she sank against the bar, feeling the weight of failure crashing down on her shoulders.

"No," she whispered to herself with a clenched fist, "I have not failed yet. And I shall not fail. Not here, not now."

BY THE TIME THE SUNS SET, Krasomila's tavern was packed shoulder to shoulder with patrons. The dining space rang with laughter, conversation, and arguments. Servers raced back and forth from the kitchens while Krasomila juggled pouring and mixing drinks, managing the register, and playing counselor for more than one sad customer. More than once, she was called to the door to instruct riders to keep their dragons from attempting to enter the establishment.

"But it's Duvarharia! Gods of old, if I wanted

to, I could go to any tavern in the Dragon Palace and my dragon could come in with me." The angry customer stood nearly two feet taller than Krasomila, his breath heavy with liquor while his dragon continued to press his snout against the door.

"Not every tavern, you *mumoželu.*" Krasomila's fists balled. "If every building in the Dragon Palace were big enough for all your oversized lizards, it'd be the size of Duvarharia itself. Now, you can either tell your dragon to wait outside, or you both can leave. Your choice, but you need to choose *now.*" A crowd was gathering around them, some trying to instigate a fight, others yelling at the customer to stop being thick headed and just leave.

The man crossed his arms, his green Shalnoa glowing vibrantly as magic raced through his blood. "I don't think I will," he slurred, swaying as he bent to her height. "I'm a rider, and I do as I please." He didn't have time to react before blood splattered on his face, the crack of a shattered nose resounding around the now silent room.

Krasomila rubbed her knuckles to dull the ache before wiping the blood off on her apron. "Get the *nufa* out of my tavern. Now."

Tears welling up in his eyes, he clutched the

fountain of blood that used to be his nose and staggered out of the tavern. His dragon's roars of shared pain filled the night until they were farther down the street, hopefully on their way home rather than to find someone else to bother.

"Krasomila?" A timid voice pipped from behind her. She turned, nose only coming up to the collarbone of the young rider. The server twiddled her thumbs. "We're out of bread."

"*Nufa!*" The foul word jumped from Krasomila's lips before she could stop it. Eyes that had once focused on the rowdy customer now turned to her. Biting her tongue, she took the server's arm and steered her through the crowd and tables and into the back kitchens. Though the chaos was overwhelming in the dining room, it was worse in the kitchens. Spices mingled in the air and tickled her nose; the ringing of metal utensils and crackling fire could barely be heard over the cooks and servers shouting at each other.

"I just baked ten dozen loaves this morning, and I've only run up five dozen. Where did the rest go?" She knew she was gripping the server's shoulders too tightly, but she couldn't care less at the moment.

"I don't know, but we're out of butter too."

"Gods!" Krasomila ripped off her apron and

tossed it in the trash before storming to the sink to wash off the rest of the blood on her hand. "Do you have any tables right now who need bread and butter?"

"All of them."

"Give them free drinks until they forget."

The young server dashed off into the crowd as if she preferred the angry customers over her frustrated boss.

Shoving her way through the kitchen, Krasomila searched everywhere for the bread she'd made. They weren't in the warm ovens, nor the bread cart, nor chilled in the ice room. Though she never put bread in the cellar because the moisture caused mold, she searched there as well; nothing.

When she staggered back up the cellar stairs, she was instantly beset upon by dozens of servers complaining about items they were out of. The cooks were yelling, saying they couldn't finish orders because of missing ingredients, and a bartender came back to announce they'd given away nearly twenty bottles of free liquor.

For the first time in the three years she'd been running the tavern, Krasomila felt her spirit snap. With a strangled sob, she turned from the mess that had once been her thriving dream. Landing a gentle hand on the first server who'd come to her, she lowered her voice and smiled through her tears. The fear in the server's eyes offered no comfort. "I'm closing the doors. Try to encourage the patrons to pay out and leave. We're closing for the night. We have nothing left." Then she made her way into the crowds, trying to plaster a smile on her face to hide the tears.

"Wait!" The server's voice called her back, and she turned only for a second. "Are you ... alright?"

A million words tripped over themselves in Krasomila's mouth, most of them lies. Instead, she whispered, "No, Anrid, no, I'm not." Then she pulled away.

Several patrons recognized her and shouted after her, demanding to hear one of her songs or stories. That's what they had come for, after all. Though the tavern's food was good and the drinks always aplenty, her fame throughout the Dragon Palace valley had grown because of her legendary tales and music. Every week, she had a new story, woven from some truth and some myth. But since the stress of losing money and products had brought up old demons she had thought buried in her past, she'd lost touch with the magic inside her that brought her stories to life.

Now she was as imagination-less as every other sorry *mumoźelu* who came to her for entertainment.

As she made her way to the tavern's doors, she could hear the servers behind her moving through the crowd, announcing their premature closure for the night, assuring the customers they would be open tomorrow.

What if that was a lie too?

Krasomila slipped outside, snatched the foldable wood sign from the pathway and threw it behind one of her bushes. Storming to the other side of the road that gave way to open sky and a straight drop cliff, she stood on the very edge and screamed into the darkness. The echoes of her voice ricocheted off the next hill city and woke a pack of dragons that took flight from the forest below.

Her chest heavy, breath suffocating in her chest, she bit back her tears and a second scream. Instead, she dropped to the ground and dangled her feet over the edge, feeling the open nothingness below her. It'd been years since she'd been at the edge of a cliff like this, feeling like she did. *What if I—*

A hand on her shoulder startled her. Barking, she scrambled back to her feet and whirled around, expecting to come face to face with an angry patron. Instead, she was staring at Metej's chest. Cursing her short ancestors, she craned her face up to meet his gaze. "What do you want?"

"I want to know why I found you at the edge of a cliff when you promised me you'd never step foot near one again."

"Metej, I run a tavern built into the sheer face of a mountain hill, what do you—"

"Shut up, Krasomila." The bite in his voice and the use of her full name banished all thoughts from her mind. "You know exactly what I'm talking about, and don't you dare joke about this. It wasn't funny the first time, it sure as Susahu wouldn't be funny the second."

Her face burned as she swallowed and nodded. "Alright," she whispered meekly, "I won't."

"The last of the customers are about to leave, and I sent the staff home. We can clean tomorrow. Right now, I want you to come back inside."

Numbly and wishing she could see his face in the dark, she didn't move his hand from her arm as he led her back to the tavern. They waited for the last of the customers to trickle out, taking their frivolity and business to the other taverns and restaurants lining the cliff face.

Once they were inside, she made her way to the large fireplace while he locked the doors. The tavern had never been so loud as it was in this silence. Plates were left on the table and chairs crooked. A bottle of *lurujmu fuju* lay on its side, a puddle of the expensive gold liquid seeping into the wood floor beneath it.

"Don't worry about it. It's just a little mess."

No mess had ever been little to Krasomila, but he knew that. Gently, he pushed her to one of the plush armchairs and gestured for her to sit down. He took a seat in the chair next to hers, leaning forward, icy eyes searching her face. She avoided looking at him, choosing instead to stare blankly into the flickering flames. She wrapped a curl of her hair around a finger, released it, then wrapped it again.

Voices she'd thought forgotten stirred in her mind as the disheveled tavern closed in on her.

"You would throw away everything we've done for you, just to run a–a–a bar *like some uneducated, lower-class wench?" Her mother's exaggerated wails filled the room, stabbing at Krasomila's heart as painfully as her father's daggered gaze.*

"We've given you hundreds of opportunities others would die for, Krasomila. Why do you insist on dragging our efforts and our family name into ruin?

You could be on the Council or bonded to a powerful well-bred dragon type and flying in the military. But you're insisting *you want to sing and serve alcohol to* sufaxab *who bond with* wild *dragons?"*

She sank into her chair, feeling smaller than a Fairy Dragon hatchling.

"I knew we should've had more children." Her mother sobbed into her hands, the chilling sound echoing off granite halls. "What a waste!"

Metej's voice shattered the memories. "Why didn't you tell me sooner?"

I was worried you'd be as disappointed as they'd been, was what she wanted to say. Instead, she only whispered, "You know why."

"I thought you said you'd changed."

She pushed herself farther into the chair, wishing it would swallow her whole. But it hadn't when she was younger, so why would it now? "I guess I was wrong."

He shook his head then sat back. "Something tripped one of my detection wards tonight, something full of its own magic."

A spark of hope flashed through her as she sat forward. "Who was it?" She thought of her old katars, tucked away in a chest, collecting dust and webs, and how she very much longed to let the violence take hold of her limbs once more and put an end to whoever was stealing from her.

"*What* is it," he corrected. "And I don't know. It's ... familiar, but unlike anything I've encountered before. But I think ..."

"What do you think?" She wanted to throttle the answer out of him.

"Well." A nervous chuckle parted his pale lips as he shrugged, playing with the end of his long braid. "If I didn't know any better, I'd say it was a dragon."

The bark of laughter that escaped her lips let him know just how ridiculous she thought that was.

"I know, Kras. I'm not a fool." His brows furrowed, and she felt a pang of guilt. He wouldn't say something so ridiculous if he wasn't absolutely sure of his findings.

"I didn't say you were."

His eyes narrowed, but he dropped the argument. *Always the peacemaker,* she thought to herself. "Why do you think it was a dragon?"

Holding out his palm, he conjured a shimmer of gold magic. Twisting and turning, the dust-like energy formed into several shapes, some looking like cats, some dogs, some riders, but it settled on the form of a dragon. Leaning closer, she searched for any defining characteristics of the dragon's type. Nothing stood out; it was the most generic dragon she'd ever laid eyes on.

"Strangely enough, I couldn't detect any specific magic type either. Whatever magic the dragon has, it either can conceal its trace immaculately, or its trace somehow blends into the tavern."

"Is it a Camouflage Dragon?"

He shook his head.

Exasperated, she flung herself back into the armchair and groaned. "Just my luck. I get the one dragon that can somehow fit into my tiny tavern, blend into the magic of the walls, and then eat all my food. Of course. I'm cursed."

She could feel his disapproving stare, but she ignored it.

"So, how do we catch the *sufax*?"

KRASOMILA PACED OUTSIDE her tavern. The two

suns were blinding without cloud cover. Winter's chill was in the air and prickled her skin. Years ago, she wouldn't have batted an eye at the oncoming freeze, but after spending more than a couple years inside the dark cave-like tavern, she'd grown sensitive to the extreme weather of Duvarharia. Metej promised the capture wards would be easy to cast and the culprit caught within a few hours, and though only one of those hours had passed, she didn't know how much longer she could wait. Already, she'd placed orders for more food, hoping to be open and running smoothly by that night, but the dining area still needed cleaning, and even with the staff coming in a few hours early, it would be a mad scramble to get back on their feet.

Then she would have to face the demanding pressure to perform stories and music. Mere months ago, that would've been what she looked forward to the most. Now just thinking about it brought back crushing memories of her disappointed family who'd wanted her to become a warrior in the Dragon Wings or a city elite, not an entertainer. Unable to conjure more than the opening of a story or two lines of mismatched poetry, she'd failed at her dream of being a storyteller. But if she could get her tavern back, at least she'd still have her dream of owning her own business where others could perform their arts.

The ground shook when a slim, white dragon landed next to her, a gust of wind mussing her already tangled hair. Grumbling, she batted the curls from her face. "Hello, Idona. What are you doing here?"

Growling, the dragon shifted her wings and shook her neck, scattering puffs of clouds to the ground. The white condensation hung unnaturally like pillows of thick fog before slowly dissipating and drifting off the cliff to join the clouds below. Idona projected her thoughts into Krasomila's mind.

I've come to give strength to my rider as he protects your tavern. I heard it's a little dragon?

Shaking her head, Krasomila turned to her tavern. From the outside, it was immaculate. Golden light from the fires and lanterns inside shone through patterned windows rimmed with iron. An awning kept guests dry on wet nights as they filtered into the tavern; upon the awning hung a sign that read *Hanluu Lure Kusos*—Sky Lake Tavern in the common tongue. She didn't want to think about what the inside looked like—messy and unkept for the first time since she bought it and refurbished it.

"That's what Metej said, but that's not possible."

Unless it's a Fairy Dragon.

Krasomila's eyes narrowed. Too often, patrons would come in with their Fairy Dragons, letting them do as they please and cause chaos. She'd never known one *not* to be spoiled rotten and downright troublesome. Though she'd never been partial to dragons, at least not in the last four years, the Fairy Dragons were the ones she liked the least. "I suppose, but it's eating a lot for such a small creature."

Idona shrugged her wings and licked her claws. *You'd be surprised.*

Before Krasomila could question her about how a dragon could hide its magic trace, Metej threw open the front doors, elation on his face. "Caught him!"

Krasomila rushed to the door and fought against Metej as he held her back. "Metej, let me go! What are you doing?"

His grip didn't loosen. "I want you to listen to me before you go rushing in there."

"It's a Fairy Dragon, isn't it?" Rage boiled in her limbs; she broke away from him.

"Yes, it is, which—no!" He wrapped his lean arms around her, easily holding her in place despite her kicking. "You can't kill it, Krasomila!

It's a dragon."

She spat to the ground and hissed, "It's no dragon to me."

Lips tickling her ear, he whispered low and dangerously. "The city elites will know the second you spilled that dragon's blood, and you would lose *everything*. You're letting your anger control you again. I thought you'd changed." The disappointment in his voice froze her limbs. She *had* changed, hadn't she? But over the last few months, it'd been harder and harder to ignore the pit of empty longing and regret that opened inside her each morning she woke, the space in the bed next to her cold and empty. No one greeted her in the kitchen when she came downstairs. No one helped her make the bread, no one helped her close the tavern at night. No one sang her music with her or helped her write her songs.

She hadn't wanted to admit it for some time, but her dream had become empty after she cut off everyone she could've shared it with. Tears collected in her eyes as familiar anxiety and dread twisted her gut. Her inability to access the storytelling magic in her blood hadn't anything to do with losing money in the tavern. It had everything to do with the demons she still struggled with from her past—demons she'd rather bury deep than face. Demons that told her to banish any reminders of that past, even the good things like Metej, the stories, and the music. Demons that had begun to whisper that same things her parents had: *Failure. Disappointment. Disgrace. Worthless.*

"I had to do it, Metej. You know that. I had to leave them. I had to leave it all."

"I know." His arms loosened around her as wisps of his baby blue hair fell into her face, his nose nudging the curve of her neck behind her ear. "But you didn't have to leave me."

No, she hadn't.

Turning and standing on her tiptoes, she threaded her arms around his neck and pulled him down into her embrace. Tears flowed down her cheeks as she bit her lip, staring at the ceiling before closing her eyes. His body was warm, familiar against hers, bringing back memories of what life had been like when she'd let him into her life and heart. It had been his music, joy, and confidence that had given her the courage to chase her dream and set herself free. When her family left her, casting her to the streets because she didn't meet their expectations or conform to their desires, Metej had been there. He was always proud of her and had never expected more than she could give. Even when she left him to find herself and her own path, he'd encouraged her, promising to always be just a dragon's flight away if she needed anything. And when he'd sat at her bar years later, he hadn't asked for anything other than a drink in exchange for coin. She didn't know how she'd ever lost sight of the fact that her dream had always included him too.

"Are you going to kill it? Because if you're hugging me so I drop my guard, I'm already waiting for you to bolt. You're not getting away."

True laughter burst from her lips as she shook her head. "No, gods, I'm not going to kill the *sufax*. I guess I'll have to save Fairy Dragon stew for another day." He must've heard the sincerity in her voice because he drew away first, a familiar, sly smile on his face.

"I suppose I am just that charming, aren't I? Maybe a touch irresistible?"

Rolling her eyes, she pulled her curls back and wrangled them in place with a square of cloth. "Actually, I think I liked it better when we had a bar between us and the noise of the crowd to drown out your voice."

"If that's what you prefer." He held out his hands and made a show of turning to the door. "I suppose I could also just let the dragon loose again—"

"Get over yourself, Metej. Come on." Heart racing in her chest and more nervous than she cared to admit, Krasomila made her way to the kitchen doors. "Maybe I'll kill him after all," she chuckled as her shaking hand hesitated to push open the door.

"We'll see," was all that Metej answered.

With a strange hum in her veins, pulling her in, dragging her towards the kitchen, Krasomila opened the door and stepped inside. The noise in her mind grew louder, sounding like hundreds of voices speaking all at once. The chatter would've been overwhelming to anyone else, but to her, it was the sound of music. Tears filled her eyes. She hadn't heard the unorganized lyrics and stories for so long. Hearing it now felt like taking a breath after drowning.

When she moved into the main cooking space, she found the source of the music.

Struggling against chains of gold magic wrapped around his legs and wings, a Fairy Dragon the size of a large dog screeched angrily and snapped its jaws. When Krasomila stepped closer, it stopped chewing on the chains and lifted its gaze to meet hers.

It was like looking into a mirror.

All at once, the noise funneled into a stream of coherent thought and music, perfectly composed, ready to be sung, played, written down. The music was coming from the dragon, filling Krasomila and bringing out the music in her that had been crushed by old fears and demons.

Focused entirely on the small dragon who now stood completely still, Krasomila was hardly aware of Metej as he waved his hand, dissipating the magic chains.

Though freed, the dragon stepped closer instead of away. He was where he wanted to be. And so was Krasomila. Reaching out a hand, she knelt and waited until the little dragon crept closer. He hesitated before touching his nose to her skin.

"I'm sorry for cursing at you and chasing you with magic and threatening to kill you."

The little dragon's eyes narrowed, and for a moment, she thought it would turn up its nose and stalk away. Then it chirped and rubbed its face all over her hand like a feline looking for snuggles.

An overwhelming rush of warmth and comfort flooded Krasomila as her mind and soul bonded with the dragon. All its thoughts, memories, and intentions flooded into her. Now she knew why the dragon's magic had blended into the tavern. It was the same as her own—the magic of storytelling. Tears trickled down her cheeks as the dragon jumped into her arms, licking her face, nibbling on her fingers, and wrapping his wings around her.

"A Muse Fairy Dragon. One of the rarest." Metej laughed as she staggered to her feet, only barely able to pick up the chunky dragon. He'd certainly been eating well the last month.

I was hungry. The dragon's small tenor voice trilled in Krasomila's mind, and she nearly dropped him in surprise. The sensation of this dragon's thoughts in hers was far different than other dragons simply projecting their thoughts. The other dragons' thoughts sounded like words spoken regularly; this dragon's thoughts sounded like they were coming from her own mind.

"I know you were. You still are." Laughing, she heaved the dragon higher into her arms as she met Metej's sparkling gaze.

Metej placed a hand on his chest and bowed. "I'd like to formerly introduce myself as Metej, rider of Idona the Imagination Dragon. May the suns smile upon your presence."

The Faïry Dragon's thoughts rang through Krasomila's mind before projecting into Metej's.

As do the stars sing upon yours. I am Senua, a Muse Fairy Dragon. Then he turned his attention to Krasomila. *I traveled across Duvarharia to find a legendary storyteller to inspire. When I felt the magic inside your blood slipping into darkness, I came to inspire you and your magic so you can once again awe the Duvarharians with your stories. I came for you, Krasomila.*

"And to eat?" Krasomila raised a brow at the little purple and navy dragon as he licked his lips.

That too.

"You nearly cost me my tavern." She scowled, but he was unbothered, his shining eyes blinking mischievously.

How else was I to get you to open your heart to the people you love?

THAT NIGHT, THE TAVERN WAS PACKED to the brim. The previous night's drama seemed to draw in more customers, many of whom wanted good food and drink while they listened to gossip about last night's events. Fairy Dragons fluttered around the vaulted ceilings and support beams, stealing food from other customers and causing chaos; for the first time, they didn't bother Krasomila.

Warmth from the fire spread throughout the room, into the dancing or sitting bodies and into their hearts, lifting their spirits high with the endless drinks and second courses.

Krasomila was behind the bar as usual, sliding chilled shots or full, frothing horns of drinks across the bar. The sound of horns and glasses clashing into each other among cheers mingled with the metal *clank* of the register.

Senua chirped and licked the froth off a patron's drink while he wasn't looking. Krasomila shot him a dirty look, but he only licked his lips mischievously. Purple magic twined from his body to the man, giving him inspiration to embellish the hunting trip he was telling a tale about. Laughter from the group rang loudly, and Krasomila shook her head. Happy customers brought more sales, so she didn't scold her Muse Dragon. They were perfect for each other—wild, creative, and always looking for a good time.

Her heart swelled when she looked out across the rowdy crowd as they shared her dream with her—a gathering place where everyone was welcome, where one could partake in the simple joys of life, forget about the expectations of others, and find new friends in the company of strangers.

It's a beautiful dream. You have done well. Senua nuzzled Krasomila's hand until she spared him a scratch behind the head.

You nearly ruined it.

His eyes pierced into hers, full of annoyance. *No, your inability to face your past, realize the mistakes you made by pushing everyone away, and stop identifying as a disappointment—which you are not—are what almost ruined it. I just ate some food and brought back your spark.*

Laughing, she pressed a kiss to his forehead. He wasn't wrong. With an excited chirp, he flew off to inspire yet another ridiculous tale and steal someone else's food.

Then just when she didn't think the night could get any better, she heard a sound she hadn't for years, a sound that brought butterflies to her stomach—an accordion. The crowd roared in excitement as they pushed Metej to a table and he clambered on top of it. Pleads for specific songs or tales filled the room, each vying for his attention, for his favor. Instead, his eyes searched for Krasomila.

When their gazes locked, he smiled his sly

grin and pulled out a few strands of baby blue hair from his braid. "Well?" he mouthed.

Shaking her head, Krasomila laughed and mouthed back, "How could I say no?" Then she grabbed her lyre from where she'd stashed it months ago under the bar and brushed the dust and cobwebs from it. The crowd parted for her as she made her way to Metej. Hiking up her layered skirts, she climbed up onto the table beside him. From up there, she felt like a ruler—a ruler over her own little world and dream.

"Welcome back, Kras." He winked at her, and a broad grin spread across her face.

Then with her lover's eyes locked on hers, inspiration from her dragon filling her mind, and her own storytelling gift filling her veins, she set the music free.

SILENCE OF SLEEP IN A FOREST SO DEEP

Trans-Falls, Ravenwood
Year: Rumi 5209 Q.RJ.M

MANY CREATURES ENTER FORESTS hoping to find solace and silence, but those who live in the woods know silence is the sound of death. For Keziah, the oppressive silence was the most wretched thing she'd ever heard.

Stepping gingerly over sticks and fallen branches, Keziah avoided stepping on anything that would shatter the silence. As much as she hated it, she felt it'd be blasphemous to disrupt it. She wasn't the only one; she'd seen the other Centaurs avoiding the stone walkways throughout Trans-falls lest their hooves clatter against them. The city itself seemed dead in the silence, and out here in the thick of the woods, Keziah was painfully aware of how very alone she was—how very alone they all were.

Eyes catching sight of a blue shimmer, Keziah changed her path and picked her way to the small growth of elusive *zheborgiy* fungus. They were higher up the tree trunk than she could reach. Painfully, she remembered how easy it used to be to simply ask the tree for help. Now when she looked at the bark, it remained lifeless, motionless, as still as death. Pressing a hand to the tree's rough skin, she wondered if it could feel her still or if it was completely lost in the dark world of sleep.

"Forgive me," she whispered before rearing up, hooves landing against the bark as she reached for the mushrooms. *A little farther* ... Just barely, her fingers wrapped around the shrooms, and she pulled, separating them from their life source. A shiver ran down her spine as she dropped back to the ground, tucking the fungus into her herb basket. It felt wrong to take from the tree without asking first.

But now she didn't have any way of speaking to them, not since ...

A wave of naseua washed over her as memories she'd rather not remember flooded her mind.

The sky had been dark for days, throwing

Trans-Falls into chaos and disorder. Armies of Warriors had been sent out to find the cause of the darkness. Ambassadors from all over Ventronovia had rushed to find the source. They'd found it had started in the heart of Ravenwood by a Centaur Trans-Falls had called their own.

Bumps rose along Keziah's arm, and she shivered, though the breeze was warm. On the last day of darkness, the sky had rent open. Beings with unfathomable, shifting forms, frighteningly similar to the Etas, moved through the sky, waiting to cross the gap between Rasa and Hanluurasa, the sky realm. Hundreds of eyes had shone down, watching, waiting, full of hunger. Then a wave of magic exploded across the land, bending trees, tearing apart homes, and even killing several Centaurs.

One moment, the forest had been alive and teeming with nymphs, Fauns, and walking trees. The next, they were all gone.

Tears collected in Keziah's eyes as she remembered watching the forest slip beneath the Sleeping, how she'd run to Phyllida's tree and watched as her nymph friend curled into its roots, closed her eyes, and promised she was only taking a nap. Keziah hadn't seen her since.

When the memories faded, Keziah found herself staring at the same tree—a delicate weeping willow with long, spindly branches flowing in the breeze. No other movement rippled through its boughs.

Ducking under the strings of leaves and branches, Keziah dragged her hooves to the tree's trunk, touching the bark where Phyllida's face had once been with petals for eyes and leaves for lips. Now it was faceless—no different than any other nymph-less tree.

"When will you wake? How long will I have to wait?"

Before the Sleeping, Keziah had spent her days running through the forest with Phyllida, chasing handsome tree nymphs, swimming in the streams with the river nymphs, and collecting ingredients for Keziah's healing class. They'd been young, carefree back then, hardly worrying about the state of the world, simply making the most of each warm sun ray and cold river.

In one day, Keziah had been forced to grow up, to leave behind the childish laughter and games. As a healer, she'd been called to duty for Trans-Falls. The Sleeping hadn't just affected the forest; it'd damaged the Centaurs as well. After all, the trees and Fauns were brethren to the Centaurs. Now she spent almost all her free time tending to those weakened by the curse hanging over the forest.

Her fingers tightened around the blue *zheborgiy* fungus she'd collected. It seemed such a small amount compared to the hundreds who lay sick or wounded and in need of ingredients like it. She was lucky she was young; the older Centaurs like her father hadn't been able to recover from the dark magic's presence as quickly; some hadn't survived at all.

Trying to keep her hands from shaking, Keziah removed three small *Leño-zhego* flowers from her basket and laid them at the base of the tree. "I know you're only sleeping, but it feels like you've died." Though she knew an answer wouldn't come, disappointment stabbed her heart with the silence anyway. "But that's alright. I promise I'll be here when you wake up. The Igentis is already looking for the *Zelauwgugey*, the Lyre of the Forest's Essence. He says it could bring you back. I know it will." She pressed her lips to the trunk, smelling the wood, the leaves, and wishing she could smell the blossoms that once grew in the leaves. "Soon. We'll be together again soon."

Turning, she ducked back under the willowing branches, believing for a moment that they wrapped around her a little tighter, as if holding her there. Then they fell lifeless again. Swallowing her hope, Keziah walked back into the forest to finish collecting the ingredients she would need for her dark magic repelling potion her father needed. All the while, she whispered the potion's spell under her lips, searching for the small magic residing in her mind. The more she practiced, the stronger she could make the potion and the more likely her father was to recover—the more likely all the older Centaurs were to recover.

They needed to survive, they needed to carry on the stories of the forest, to speak of a time when the trees waved their branches like arms, laughed with breath smelling of sap and spring, and how their spirits would step from their physical bodies and run through the forest, making mischief, and blessing the land with new growth wherever they crossed. Someone needed to speak of the Fauns and their wild parties, and the beat of their drums, and the trill of their flutes. Someone needed to carry stories and legends they told of great beings who once walked Rasa and Haluurasa, shaping the very world and sky, and of star beings who came down from Haluurasa to fuse their spirits into the forest.

Keziah tightened her fists with determination. Though the forest was as silent as death now, it didn't have to stay that way ... not forever. Until someone found the *Zelauwgugey* Lyre and banished the dark magic, Keziah promised to bring the noise back, to bring the *life* back.

As she made her way home, she walked on the stone road, hooves striking loudly against the rock, echoing through the silent forest. In the distance, she almost believed she heard a Faun's drum answer.

DREAMING OF FREEDOM AND PASTRIES

Sichas, Sorcolle
Year: Rumi 4049 Q.RJ.M

A CREAKING DOOR REGISTERED somewhere in the back of Nescres's mind, but she dismissed it. Fleeting specks of white snow drifted from the heavens, captivating her attention and melting as soon as they touched the ground. Small puddles formed in the red dirt roads and darkened the adobe buildings; the snow refused to stick into fluffy piles.

With a deep sigh, Nescres leaned her forehead against the cold glass and blew against it, watching it fog. "Citana?" she whispered. Her handmaiden's hooves padded softly on the thick carpet until Nescres could feel her standing just beside her, the warmth of her body opposite to the cold of the window.

"Yes, Nescres?"

The words she'd wanted to say stuck in her throat as she turned her focus back to the windows. A colossal set of stone staircases led down to the next tier of the pyramid-like palace she lived in, or rather, felt trapped in.

"Nescres, my star, you must stay here for your protection," she remembered one of her fathers saying. *"You are beautiful. Beauty is value, and value is irresistible to the greedy. Your place is here, in the palace, waiting to serve the next Kings."*

So in the palace she stayed, day after day, night after night, taught only how to be beautiful, to be desirable, to be the next Queen of Socrolle. But she longed for more, and on this cold afternoon, she wasn't sure she could deny her heart any longer. Finally, she whispered, "I want to go outside."

Nescres felt Citana stiffen, but the handmaiden didn't lash out. Though it was Citana's duty to keep the Princess safe, Nescres knew she had once been free and desired to be free once again. Citana stayed quiet as Nescres's words faded into silence, neither reprimanding nor agreeing.

"At least tell me about Ravenwood." Nescres

pressed a hand to the window, imagining the mysterious northern land where Centaurs were ruled by Chiefs in tribes rather than three Kings in an empire. She'd heard it described as a land full of cold, white peaked mountains and of oak and maple trees that changed colors in autumn. A land where females could fight in the military and own land, where they were worth more than just their beauty. A land where Centaurs mated for love.

"I've told you all I remember. You know I was very young when ..." Citana's voice tapered off as she moved closer to the window. The same longing hung in her eyes as she peered across Sichas Ema ar Gis, the city of power, then to the tropical forest beyond. Already the snow had stopped falling; it would be the most winter they'd see all year. If they were lucky, the wind would bring the north's cold for a few more weeks before relentless summer bore down upon them again.

"I know, but I want to hear it again. I want to hear about your family's bakery."

A small smile cracked Citana's lips. Though she never spoke much about the family she lost, she never passed up the chance to reminisce of their bakery. "They opened it in a beautiful little cabin nestled deep in the center of our tribe on one of the busiest streets."

"Was the tribe built from stone?" Nescres looked out over her own city. Every building was either constructed of giant gray stones pulled from the nearby quarries or slathered with red adobe and thatched with dried plant life. When the Centaur settlers first arrived, they'd leveled a portion of the thick jungle until bare land remained. Thousands of years later, Sichas still fought the forest; all expansion demanded the jungle's destruction, and with each new section built, they erected another wall to keep the forest out.

"No; it was mostly built of wood and intertwined with the trees. It was covered in vines, flowers, and berry bushes. The trees' spirits walked through the woods, and wherever their feet touched, vegetation would spring and grow. Their laughter filled the silence, and you could always make dozens of new friends just by stepping outside your door. Anytime trees were needed for construction, the tree spirts were consulted so the health of the forest and spirits were preserved."

"They respected the forest."

"Always."

With a heavy sigh, Nescres closed her eyes and tried to imagine living in a forest where the trees grew so big and far apart that entire tribes existed under the leafy canopy—a world existing in harmony with nature, rather than against it. She'd have to see it for herself someday. "Do you miss them?" she whispered. "Your family, I mean?"

"Of course, but ..." Gently, Citana combed her fingers through Nescres's straight hair, tucking a small braid behind her ear. "I have you."

"But I'm not your family." Nescres tried to imagine what having a loving, caring family would be like. The closest she could relate it to were the days before her mother's death when she and her three fathers sometimes spent a dinner laughing instead of in silence or with raised voices.

"Maybe not by blood, but the same stars run through our veins. That makes us family more than anything else."

Smiling, Nescres nodded and leaned into Citana's touch.

A sharp rap on the door disrupted the still silence they'd fallen into. Nescres hardly stirred as Citana answered the door, speaking in low tones with the visitor. Nescres almost hoped it was one of her fathers, but nearly four years had passed since one of them had come to see her. A small ping of disappointment rang in her heart when the door closed and Citana said it was only a delivery.

The tearing of paper and a quiet hum filled the room as the handmaiden opened the letter and quickly skimmed through it.

"Who's it from?" Nescres expected it to be dinner summons; no one else wrote to her, unless it was one of her tutors asking her to class.

"King Chunid."

Interest slightly piqued, Nescres uncurled her legs and stood, taking a moment to stretch. Though the Socrolle gods insisted no parent be favored over the other, Nescres couldn't help but secretly prefer Chunid. Where Aaris was frightening and Gamo was indifferent, Chunid always held some interest in their only daughter; he was the only one she remembered possibly loving her mother.

"It's an announcement of the Kings' departure to the city of Blarta for the first competition of the new elite military." Her eyebrows rose as she quietly read the letter again.

A shiver of excitement flooded Nescres's veins. "I thought that wasn't for another moon cycle." She rushed to Citana's side to peek over her shoulder, though the handmaiden, nearly a head taller, held the letter just out of reach.

"They weren't."

"When are they leaving?"

"Noon of today. An hour ago. They're already gone."

Perhaps she should've been upset that her fathers left without a proper goodbye, but a million other thoughts and a single driving plan whirled through Nescres's mind instead.

"I'm not expected for temple lessons until next week, after which I'll be under guard for the next eight moon cycles. Then is my sixteenth life ritual and the announcement of my becoming Queen once the new Kings are chosen. I'll have the entire temple guard and priests watching over me after that." Nescres cantered around the room as she gathered what she needed to put her plan into motion.

"Nescres, what are you doing?" Though hesitancy laced Citana's voice, Nescres also heard the hint of excitement.

"Citana," she stopped before her handmaiden and took her hands. "I know you want this as much as I, so don't try to stop me. Enjoy this with me. *Please.*" She would do this with or without Citana's help, but Citana was her whole world.

To do anything without her felt empty, pointless.

"Nescres, we can't just *leave*. You're safe here. If you go out there ..." Citana nodded to the windows. "Who knows what would happen? Neither of us know how to fight. And if your fathers or the priest ever found out ..." She shivered.

Nescres's grip tightened on hers; she wished Citana wasn't right. "I know. That's why we're not really leaving. We're just going into the city. I just want to see it, to experience it, just once."

The longing in Citana's eyes gave away her answer. "But what about your markings? Even if they don't recognize you as the Princess, the slavers will hunt you for your markings."

With a sly smile, Nescres waved a bottle of black liquid under Citana's nose. "Already thought of that."

Citana's eyes widened. "Is that ...?"

"Dye from the temple? Yes. I slipped it from a sleeping priest."

Clear laughter ran through the room and lit a new spark in Nescres's heart. "Someday you're going to get yourself killed." Citana chuckled despite her dark words.

"Dying trying to live would be better than just

surviving. Now, help me get these spots covered."

The process of getting the black dye onto Nescres's white spots without staining every inch of the white limestone washroom proved much more difficult and time consuming than Nescres had anticipated.

Since the dye was for ritual markings on sacrifices or for the priests, not for dying large amounts of skin or hair, the contents of the bottle only covered Nescres's legs, stomach, and tail. The rest of her white and black spotted body would have to be hidden with the torn cloak she'd scavenged from the palace's discards a couple of years ago.

She surveyed herself in the mirror and nodded. As long as she kept her head down and did nothing to draw attention, they'd remain hidden just long enough to explore Sichas for a couple hours before the suns set. They'd need to be back in the temple palace before dark; the guard would notice her absence if she didn't show for dinner. Though it wasn't nearly as much time as she'd dreamed, any time outside was more than she'd had the last seven years or than she'd get for the rest of her life.

Nearly two hours after receiving the letter, they were finally ready. The last obstacle between them and the start of their adventure was the door.

As Citana reached for the door handle, she hesitated and whispered, "Are you sure you want to do this?" Though her words ignited panic in Nescres, she saw only excitement and eager longing when their eyes met. Citana was ready; she only wanted to make sure her Princess was too.

But doubt crept into her mind as a memory washed over her.

"You are beautiful, Nescres. Beautiful enough to be the next Queen of Socrolle." King Chunid smiled as he tucked a lock of her white and black hair behind her ear. "You have the markings of your mother, the markings of our ancestors, children of the gods."

The echoes of her hooves striking stone reverberated through the temple as she danced in excitement.

"But ..." The hesitation in his voice halted her celebration. "But that means you can never leave the palace."

Her excitement immediately dissolved into horror. "Never?"

Slowly, he shook his head. "Never. Not until you're Queen and have produced another beautiful Queen."

Tears stung her eyes. "But why?"

His large, warm hands encircled hers. "Because

out there, creatures would try to exploit you for themselves, to enslave you and your beauty, to make wealth off your body. Socrolle needs you here, in the palace, to be a beautiful figurehead decended for them to look up to."

"But I want to rule like you do! I want to go fight and build things and see the sea!" Her teeth chewed at her lip.

His voice was firm. "A Queen's place is not to rule. It is at the hooves of her husbands, the Kings." He sighed heavily, then drew her close. "The Kings lead and serve the land. But who will serve the Kings if not the Queen? You must offer your life to them, so they have what they need to rule powerfully. This is the sacrifice you must make for the kingdom. This is your destiny."

She threw her little arms around his torso and cried until she had no more tears left.

Like any young Centaur of nine years, she'd believed every word he said, letting the seed of fear and desolation take root in her heart. That day and every day since, she'd been reminded that her dreams were not her own and neither was her life. The palace owned her, and the only way for them to keep her safe was to imprison her.

Tears glistened in her eyes as the memory faded. Subconsciously, her fingers trailed her face.

Her markings were the same as her mother's—not uncommon in their country Socrolle, but coveted, nonetheless. Since her mother's bloody death four years ago, she'd believed what her fathers told her: her mother was killed in a kidnapping attempt. But the more years that passed, the more she remembered hidden details of that dark day, and no longer did she feel she could trust everything her fathers told her to believe. Especially when they insisted she was only worth being a figurehead. "Do you think the outside world is as bad as my fathers say?"

Citana turned, shock on her face. "Why do you ask that? Of course, it is."

Guilt pierced Nescres's heart. *Of course, it is.* Citana—torn from her lovely baker family in Ravenwood and sold to slavers in Socrolle—was a perfect example of the world's cruelty.

But wasn't being stolen from the land and life you love the same as being locked in a temple and kept from seeing the land and life you could have?

Tears gathered in Nescres's eyes as she reached for Citana's hand. Their fingers intertwined and tightened fiercely around each other. "Just once. I only want to be free just once. Then I'll be the Princess and Queen they want me to be."

A strange emotion crossed Citana's face, but

before Nescres could decipher it, she brought her small hand to her lips and kissed it. "Just once," she echoed softly.

Then they stepped through the door.

"I'M NOT SURE THIS WILL WORK." Hesitation and fear filled Citana's eyes as she adjusted Nescres's cloak hood for seemingly the hundredth time, trying to tuck back wisps of white and black hair and hide the spots on Nescres's face.

Nescres waved her away then tugged her elbow length gloves farther up her arms. A guard turned down the hall just ahead.

Nescres quickly turned her face, hoping he hadn't recognized her. "It has to work," she hissed quietly. "I'm not turning back now."

The guard passed by them without a second glance. They released a long sigh of relief.

Wrapping her cloak tighter around her, Nescres surveyed her surroundings, marveling at how much colder the servant halls were compared to the central temple and royal quarters. She was thankful Citana's room was next to hers and always warm. Though excited to see new walls, rooms, and Centaurs for the first time in years, Nescres made sure to focus on the journey, committing each turn to memory. Should the need ever arise, she wanted the route to the city to be a quick thought away.

With more ease than she'd expected, they came to the final doors, stopped behind a line of servants waiting for permission to leave the temple.

When it came their turn, Nescres remained silent like she'd promised. Citana showed the guard her royal servant's seal and explained they were the Princess' servants on their way to obtain new fabric for the Princess' wardrobe. The guard waved them on without batting an eye.

Since she'd been born to the three Kings and the Queen of Socrolle, Nescres had always known she was above the rest of the world, even before she'd been selected to be the next Queen. Now, as she experienced more freedom disguised as a servant than she ever had as Princess, she questioned how superior she actually was.

Then they were standing under the blazing warm suns, no sign of the earlier winter weather besides a few leftover puddles.

For a long moment, Nescres squeezed her eyes

shut and covered them, struggling to adjust to the blinding light. Though she was allowed into the temple garden, the suns had been dimmed by the courtyard's great dome of glass.

"Are you alright?" Citana's soft hand on her shoulder encouraged her to try peering into the bright streets once again. The light wasn't as overwhelming this time, and she quickly forgot the pain's memory once she took in the sights of Sichas.

Great stone steps stretched down below them, full of servants coming to and from the step pyramid, some with empty baskets, others with full baskets strapped to their horse backs or balanced on their shoulders and heads.

The city reverberated with the clamor of hundreds of hooves on stone and the shouts of bargaining in the marketplace. The colors of fabrics and paint were far more vibrant to the bare eye than seen through a thick window. It created the most beautiful rainbow she had ever seen.

Packing the streets were hundreds of booths with colorful sunshades; some connected to adobe stores behind them, others covered traveling merchants. The fruits and products the tradesmen were selling displayed as many patterns and colors as their sunshades. Nescres wondered how anyone could decide on what to buy when faced with so many beautiful options.

She reached for Citana's hand and squeezed, her heart racing. She wanted to stay here forever, just watching the world move on below her; but she also wanted to be *a part* of it.

Then the most wonderful smell wafted to her nose.

"We could start with the market. It's open until the fourth shadow hour after noon."

Nescres already knew where she wanted to go, but the words stuck in her throat as tears of joy rose to her eyes.

"It's alright if you're overwhelmed. There's a lot to see."

"No," Nescres laughed through the tears. She sniffed and wiped her tears on her cloak corner. "I know exactly where I want to go."

"DANCING TREE BAKERY." Nescres breathed out the store's name with as much tender love as if it were her mate. Taking in a deep breath, she tried to put names to all the spices and fruity smells swirling in the air but found the task impossible. The only word she could give was: "Perfect."

Citana squeezed her hand. A broad grin spread across her face as tears sparkled in her eyes, mirroring the ones in Nescres's. "Shall we?"

Nescres almost didn't want to go inside, as if by doing so, the dream would be shattered, and she'd find herself back in the palace. *But I'm really here,* she reminded herself. *This isn't just a dream.* Before she could overthink it anymore, she grabbed the handle and pulled the door open.

A bell on the door rang as heat and fragrance hit them like a thick wall.

They stepped inside, and immediately Nescres noticed how soft and forgiving the floor was under her hooves; upon closer examination, the realized floor was made of pressed cork. By the look of surprise on Citana's face, Nescres knew she noticed it too.

But the cork floors weren't the only wonders. Spanning the walls were very low tables in the middle of small sunken pits. The small pits were lined with all manners of plush throws, pillows, and furs, some of which she knew were imported from the north. Citana's eyes lingered on the furs with wistful nostalgia.

The tables in the center of the room were higher and surrounded with smaller cushions—perfect for short-term seating.

"I've never seen a bakery with seating before," Citana whispered in her ear. "I love the concept."

Nescres didn't have any prior bakery experience to compare this one to, but that only made the experience more magical. Toward the back of the room, counters and a glass display spanned the length of the wall. They moved through the cozy seating and neared the counter. Nescres gasped in delight; the display was full of delectable pastries and breads.

Citana tisked and pulled on her shoulder. With wide eyes, Nescres stepped back; she hadn't realized she'd pressed her hands and face to the glass, trying to get as close to the delicious food as she could. "Sorry," she apologized as a blush warmed her cheeks. Citana only laughed.

Then a deep, shaky voice filled the air. "Welcome! What can I help you colts with?"

Nescres looked up to see the oldest Centaur she'd ever laid eyes on. Her mane and tail were completely silver and trailed all the way to the cork floors, thick with braids and jewelry. Though her skin was wrinkled and her limbs thin, a certain strength still hovered in them as if they hadn't seen the last of hard work. The words she'd spoken held an oddly familiar accent just subtle enough she couldn't put her hoof on it. Then she became acutely aware that the bakery had gone silent, and both the baker and Citana were looking expectantly at her.

Her words tripped over themselves as they fought their way from her mouth. "I was—actually if I could—sorry, this is my first time trying a bakery, I mean being *in* a bakery. I've tried baked goods before, obviously. I mean not *obviously*, I—"

Citana's hand on her shoulder quieted her. "What my friend is trying to say is this is her first time coming into a bakery. I'm afraid she's only ever seen pastries on a table before; she hasn't even been in a kitchen, let alone a full bakery."

A crinkled smile spread across the Centaur's face as she clapped her hands, a cloud of tan flour scattering through the air. Pointing to a blackboard behind her, she rattled off some of her favorite menu items. "All prices and flavors are on the board. My name is Athena, and if you want a different glaze on one of the pastries, let me know! I'll take your order in just a moment; I'm in the middle of getting a new batch of dough into the ovens if you don't mind."

"Not at all. I'm sure we'll need lots of time to decide."

Before Athena retreated to the dough, Nescres finally recognized the hint of accent in her voice. "You're from Ravenwood!"

The Centaur woman slowly turned, sudden ice in her eyes, spiking fear through Nescres's heart. Then she remembered Centaurs from Ravenwood were illegal in Socrolle except as slaves or owned servants like Citana. Horror churned her stomach as she realized the implications of her assumption. "I'm so sorry. I didn't mean—"

Then a sly smile tugged on Athena's lips. "We all have secrets to keep, don't we, *Princess*?"

Nescres's mouth dropped as the Centaur baker trotted through the large door into a mostly covered courtyard.

"Citana—" Nescres reached for Citana, but she only laughed. "Citana, this isn't funny! She knows who I am! She'll call the palace, and they'll come for us and punish me." Nescres's hands strayed to her back where memories of old punishments began to burn once again. *My fathers were right. It's too dangerous for me out here. Perhaps it is worth living like a prisoner as long as I remain safe.*

"Nescres, you're overthinking it." Citana's laugh snapped her from her spiraling thoughts. "She'll keep your secret as long as you keep hers."

Though her heart slowed its race, the dread of guards or slavers bursting through the bakery doors at any moment remained. She didn't want this beautiful, wild day to end so soon, and neither did she want to experience the corded whip of her fathers' wrath or the tight shackles of slavery. But only she and Citana occupied the bakery, and they would be safe so long as they returned home before sunset.

"Now, pick what you want."

All thought of potential danger fled her mind as she searched through the seemingly endless number of pastry and bread options. Not only were there several different flavors per pastry type, but each bread had different herbs, spices, or shapes and options of dough. More than once, Nescres had to get Citana's help to pronounce some of the foreign Ravenwood terms for the food as well as explain what some of the spices or flavorings tasted like. She didn't know pastries could have so many different fruits in them. The Kings of Sichas' temple palace usually preferred their bread plain, and though they had their fair share of pastries, the lack of a Queen had caused the sweetness and flavors of the pastries to be lacking.

"Did you find something you want to try?" Athena had returned, minus her flour covered apron.

Nescres's eyes set on a small triangular pastry that seemed flakey like a biscuit. Citana said it was a sweet and sour citrus *woy-yulu kakezh*—a type of unsweetened bread pastry. But she'd also called it a different name that danced through Nescres's mind—*faykami.* When Nescres questioned Citana on the word's meaning, she'd laughed and said her family had called them that because their shape looked like colt hooves. Of all the names Citana read off the board, Nescres remembered *faykami* the most. Nodding, she pointed to it rather than try to repronounce its name and make a fool of herself.

Athena nodded appreciatively and slid the glass doors open, reaching in with wooden tongs to fish out one of the *faykami*. She then delicately arranged it on a plate.

"What kind of glaze would you like?"

Nescres's mind fell blank as her eyes roved across the long list of glaze flavors on the blackboard. She didn't know what half of them tasted like let alone which flavors would pair best with the fruit in her pastry.

"I recommend the *dore* citrus glaze with cane sugar. It'll pair nicely with the scone you've chosen."

Nescres nodded, then looked to Citana for approval. The handmaiden laughed and stomped a hoof. "It's your pastry, not mine. Pick whatever you want."

"I'll take the one you mentioned. Thank you." Nescres's voice sounded very young and small. In the palace, her voice demanded respect. Here, she was simply another Centaur girl wanting a sweet pastry. Somehow, she found the simplicity of this disguise suited her quite well. The palace expected her to be an exotic beauty worthy of a Queen, but here she could taste the simple freedom of childhood.

"Delightful. And for you?"

Citana put in an order for something she called a *esgren cuebre*—a small, fluffy cake with a hole in its center—and ended up choosing the same glaze Nescres did. She also ordered a drink she called *muluk* and described as herbal leaves steeped in warm water. Nescress thought it sounded like the familiar hot cocoa she drank in the palace, but Citana assured her it was entirely different.

As Athena pushed a few metallic buttons on a strange machine then read out a total, Nescres realized she hadn't brought any money. In fact, she didn't have any money at all. Everything she owned was tied to the palace. The blood drained from her face as she sputtered.

"I'm sorry, I didn't ... I forgot that I'd—" Everything she tried to say either sound painfully ignorant or extremely rude. She shut her mouth and ducked her head in shame.

"Don't worry, Nescres." Citana gently nudged her and from her belt pulled a small purse that jingled with metal. "A servant never goes anywhere without a few coins for her Princess."

Nescres' face raged with a blush. Deep down, she had a horrible feeling the coin wasn't from the palace treasury, but rather Citana's own meager savings. Athena must've known it too; as Citana counted the gold and silver coins, the old Centaur woman reached out and gently closed Citana's fingers around the coins.

"Don't worry about it."

"But—"

The baker wagged her finger under Nescres's nose. "No. I said it once, and I won't say it again. I only ask that when you become Queen, you will remember the kindness you were given by two Ravenwood Centaurs."

Emotion choked Nescres' throat. As Queen, she would have no more legal power to change the fate of illegal or enslaved Ravenwood Centaurs than they had themselves—her fathers had made it quite clear her title was only honorary—but she could remember Athena and Citana's kindness. She *would* remember their kindness. Always. With a curt nod, she settled the deal.

They were instructed to find a place to sit and ended up choosing one of the sunken couches by the wall. The adobe rock was blessedly cool, and the lack of windows gave Nescres' eyes relief from the blinding suns she still wasn't used to.

In only a few minutes, Athena had decorated their pastries with glaze and a few shavings of citrus rinds. On a cork tray, she brought them to the table, along with a steeping mug.

As soon as the plates touched the table, the *faykami* was in Nescres' hands and between her lips, an explosion of citrus and sugary delight filling her mouth with the most pleasing combination of flavors. A heavy sigh escaped her lips.

Citana and the baker laughed, but Nescres felt no embarrassment. Trying to take nibbles instead of monstrous bites like her first taste, she strove to make the pastry last.

Her enjoyment mirrored in Citana's eyes as

she took the lid off her large mug and brought the hot drink to her lips. Tears sparkled in her eyes. "I haven't had a good cup of *muluk* for so many years. This is wonderful."

Athena's silvery tail swished as she bowed. "I'm very pleased to hear that. I hope you continue to enjoy the rest."

Before she turned to leave, a question leapt from Nescres' lips. "Is this bakery yours?"

A strange expression came across Athena's face as she turned back and tilted her head. "In a way."

Nescres frowned around a mouthful of *faykami*. "What do you mean?"

With a heavy sigh, the Centaur baker stepped down into the lowered seating, groaning as her knees popped, and sighed when she finally settled down.

Citana's sparkling eyes peered over the rim of her mug, just as intrigued. Hands wrapped possessively around the mug, she had yet to touch her *esgren cuebre*. Nescres smiled into her own pastry.

"The bakery was originally my mate's idea. He was Socrolle."

"And you mated!" The idea of a Socrolle and Ravenwood Centaur mating was unheard of. Any instances Nescres knew of existed only in history books and always ended in bloody executions as "lessons" for any others to learn from.

She nodded slowly, eyes staring just past Nescres's head. "We did. In Ravenwood, it was acceptable. At least, it was in his tribe, as long as I didn't try to lay claim to any of Ravenwood's citizen's rights."

Nescres' brows furrowed. She'd heard many of Citana's stories about Ravenwood's scenery, myths, and some of the culture, but she didn't know much about the government. Instead of interrupting for more clarification, though, she let Athena continue.

"But my mate missed his home. He knew I loved baking, and he thought my recipes would do well here. He thought I could start a new craving with my sweet and sour pastries. I was young and in love, so I agreed, and we moved. For years, we managed to stay hidden from the palace and found our small success in the bakery." A nostalgic smile lifted her lips. "Those were some of the most wonderful years of my life." Then her smile fell.

"What happened?"

"The draft."

Nescres' stomach churned uncomfortably, and her eyes dropped, focusing on the scone.

"The draft of elites. The proving of new blood to either become the highest in the army or, if they're good enough, to become one of the next three Kings," Citana whispered, setting her mug down.

Athena nodded. "I never saw him again. His name never showed up on the draft's casualties nor winners. I'm not sure how he died or even if he did." Tears trickled down her cheeks as she folded her shaky hands on the table.

Citana placed a hand on hers, and they shared a sad smile. "I'm so sorry."

Athena shook her head. "In a way, it saved me. Had he been acknowledged as dead or missing by the palace, they would've come for his property. Now I can say any number of things about him without bringing suspicion of his death or absence. So instead of my illegal presence being discovered and the bakery taken from me, I was able to keep it." A sparkle of pride filled her eyes, sparking an empty pit of longing in Nescres.

"So, it is yours. And you make money from it?"

She nodded. "Enough to soon be able to travel back to Ravenwood. In fact, I hope to leave next year."

Nescres smiled, trying to find joy for her. But the pit inside her only grew wider. Of course, traveling took money, just like the food they were enjoying. Today had proven to her just how helpless she was without the temple. She didn't have a coin to her name, not even to buy herself a pastry, let alone travel.

But she wanted something of her own. Something to be proud of, to work at, succeed at, and even fail at. She wanted a life to live and her own people to love like Citana and this baker had once. Even if they had lost so many things, they at least had memories. Nescres ... she had nothing.

She didn't realize she was crying until Citana shook her shoulders and hugged her across the small table. "Little star, why are you crying?"

Embarrassed, Nescres shoved the last bit of the delicious scone into her mouth and sniffed. After a few seconds of chewing to get her thoughts and composure together, she answered. "I want to run a bakery." She tried not to keep crying but couldn't help it when she looked at the two Centaur women's solemn faces. "I want to have a life and people to love, and I want to make pastries and watch happy Centaurs enjoy them, and I want to work hard, and I want to fail and succeed. I want to be free; I want to live!"

She expected them to laugh at her. She felt ridiculous enough to laugh at.

But they didn't.

Instead, they nodded to one another and stood. Citana offered her hand to Nescres, helping her to her hooves.

"If you want to run a bakery, Princess, then you must first learn how one works." Athena straightened her shoulders, determination in her old eyes. "Follow me."

Hand tight in Citana's, Nescres let them lead her behind the counter and into the partially covered courtyard. Pathways of stone snaked under adobe and thatched roofing before cutting through an open expanse of dirt beneath the sky. Under the eaves sat above-ground ovens, which the baker explained were for the more delicate pastries like the *esgren cuebre* and *faykami*. The pit hearths in the dirt, however, were for large batches of bread.

Nescres dried her tears and watched with overwhelming fascination as the baker described how the pit hearths were cut into the dirt then lined with bricks. Before baking, a very hot fire was built in the small pit to heat up the rocks then left to burn out. When only hot coals were left, a small metal grate was placed over them, which the loaves sat on top of. Then the ovens were sealed with more rock, dirt, and leaves and left until the scent of the bread indicated whether they were done or not.

"It takes a keen nose and quick hands to catch the bread before it burns. I've had many years to practice." Pride shone in Athena's eyes as she pointed to a hearth pit and instructed Nescres on clearing the lid to access the bread. They arranged the hot loaves on big stone platters and carried them to another room for storage.

Next, she showed Nescres the most magical room yet.

Full of fresh fruits, flours, eggs, and even a cold box for milk and butter, this was the room where all the bread and pastry doughs were made. A huge recipe book with thick old yellow pages sat on its own pedestal next to the large island stone counter. The original color of the stone must've been dark red at one point, like the rest of the rock the city was built of, but, covered in flour as thickly as it was, it appeared more pink.

Mixing utensils filled the shelves along the

walls. Gears and handles made up some of the utensils for tasks like beating eggs. Others were as simple as wood spoons or stone cylinders with two handles for rolling out dough. Athena spread out the utensils and spoke quickly, explaining how most of the metal tools she'd brought from Ravenwood while much of the stone and wooden tools came from local Sichas merchants.

The massive amount of information threatened Nescres with a headache, but she didn't complain. Clinging to every little detail, she promised herself she wouldn't forget a single one.

When the tour commenced, the suns were already dipping low into the horizon. If Nescres and Citana wanted to make it back to the temple palace before dark, they'd have to leave now.

But as the three Centaurs stood around the door, tails swishing and hooves dancing nervously on the cork floor, it seemed none of them were ready to part ways. Though they knew Nescres would never get the chance to start her own bakery, the tour had been healing somehow, as if they'd needed it to believe that maybe someday, they'd find the freedom they longed for, no matter how impossible it seemed right now.

"Oh! Don't forget your cake." Athena grabbed the pastry from where Citana abandoned it at the table then trotted behind the counter to wrap it in thin brown paper. Citana took it graciously then peered down into her mug.

"There's a little bit left. I don't want it to go to waste, but I know I can't take the mug. Nescres, would you like to try it?"

Nodding quickly, she took the cup and downed the last sip of *muluk*. A look of repulse crossed her face as she coughed. "Oh!"

The other two Centaurs laughed.

"It's more bitter than I imagined." With a sorry smile, she handed the mug to Athena, who shook her head.

"It's best paired closely with a pastry. Some like honey in it or cane sugar. Others like it with cream."

Nescres wrinkled her nose. "I don't think I like it at all."

"I'm sure you'd like it the older you got. That's what happened for me."

"You're only a few years older than me, Citana."

"It's enough."

Their laughter faded into hesitant silence once

again.

Nescres wanted to stay here forever: where her worth could be determined by more than just her appearance, in this dream-like place where she could own something, where she could make her own coin, and be dependent only on herself. The idea was lovely, even if impossible.

With a deep sigh, she turned to Athena, pressed her palms together at her chest and bowed low—a sign of respect for royalty.

"Oh, do not do that to me." A blush raged on the old baker's face, but Nescres ignored her, maintaining the bow.

"Thank you for everything you have shown me here today. I will never forget it."

Something between hope and sadness filled the Centaur's eyes as she and Nescres embraced.

"I know, little Princess."

Then Citana said her thanks, and they stepped out of the bakery. The bell rang behind them. The dream broke.

THE STREETS FLOODED with bustling crowds on their way home from merchant or trade jobs. Many of the Centaurs were laden with burdens. Some even had carts strapped to themselves to haul their goods. But the darker the skies became, the less merchants trotted by, and the more suspicious Centaurs peered from under dark cloaks, ill intentions in their eyes.

On the way back to the temple palace's looming step pyramid, Nescres silently repeated over and over everything Athena told her, committing each little detail to memory.

The stairs back up the stone temple seemed longer than they had been going down. The servants' halls appeared smaller, colder, narrower. And for the first time in her life, Nescres realized just how small her own living quarters were compared to the expanse of the world. Claustrophobia tightened in her chest like a python.

As Citana helped wash the dye from her skin and hair and brush her long mane and tail, Nescres tried to find the meek, obedient Princess who had left the palace just a few hours before.

She couldn't find her.

As she curled up on her large sprawl of plush cushions, pillows, and blankets, resting her upper body on a small couch, head laid on her arms, she could no longer ignore the burning longing that had been ignited in her heart.

She'd said she'd only leave once then return to be the Queen she was expected to be. Just a few hours ago, she'd meant it. But the fear of the world's darkness and her fathers' wrath and expectations no longer suppressed her repulsions of being locked in the palace for the rest of her life. Whatever hardships she would face chasing her dream, obtaining her freedom would be worth it; of that, she was sure.

A plan began to form in her mind. She would have to wait extremely patiently; she'd have to be shrewd, cunning, and brave, but she could do it. After all, she was more than just a pretty face to be married to the next three Kings—a creature to be used only for her body. She would prove it.

Her future carefully laid out in her mind, not as her fathers wanted it, but as she did, she shut her eyes and sent a hopeful prayer to her gods. Then, as she finally drifted to sleep, her dreams were full of Ravenwood, of freedom, and of pastries.

A MATCHMAKING MEDIC

Trans-Falls, Ravenwood
Year: Rumi 6028 Q.RJ.M

"SLOW DOWN," JARGON GRUNTED as he heaved his overstuffed medical satchel onto his other shoulder. An angry blister stung where the leather strap had been digging relentlessly into his dark skin. "Blistersprout mixed with *kodaazeñi* and just a couple *zheborgiy*," he muttered under his breath, taking mental note of the necessary ingredients needed for a blister-healing salve. Ironically, he would be healing a wound with the remedies he carried—the very burden that caused the wound in the first place. *That seems ridiculous.*

"Jargon! Stop walking so slowly. Put some fire under your hooves! I want you to watch me shoot today." Black hooves cantered through the woods ahead of him, their rhythm quickly fading as the distance between the two Centaurs grew.

"Stars of old, Frawnden. You want me to watch you shoot every day," he grumbled, pushing his glasses farther up the bridge of his nose. After seeing her shoot hundreds of times, he almost believed she'd come from the womb with a bow and arrow in hand. But no matter what classes or competitions he observed, she always had another to drag him to.

Ducking under a low branch, Jargon squinted at the sudden burst of light. The Trans-Falls valley was almost entirely dominated by enormous trees, towering so high, they seemed to fill the sky with their leaves. But every so often, the dense forest opened into clearings. Some were small, only large enough for a small campfire, but others were vast, empty meadows, though the grassy clearing he'd just stepped into wasn't empty at all.

A large gathering of Centaur Warriors had chosen this site to set up the quintennial elite archery competition. Any Centaurs enrolled in the top archery class had a chance to enter the competition and win one of five spots on the Igentis Artigal's team of elite archers.

Though bored of being dragged to every one of Frawnden's archery classes, Jargon couldn't help but feel a surge of pride. She was the unchallenged top of the class, with only three other archers coming anywhere remotely close to her scores. Her spot on the Centaur leader's elite team was as assured as the two suns above them.

Breaking into a trot, Jargon closed the distance between them, standing just to her side as she excitedly compared arrows with two of the other top contestants.

Though ruthless in her rise to the elite archers of Trans-Falls, Frawnden had never alienated herself from her competition. If anything, she'd become a shining example of not just skill, but character as well. Yet for all her willingness to teach, laugh, and make merry, she'd steered away from developing close relationships, especially of the romantic kind. Jargon laughed as her voice rang through his mind. *"Taking a loss from someone kind hurts worse than someone rude, but taking a loss from one you consider a friend or lover I'm sure hurts the worse."*

He'd tried many times to convince her that companionship was worth the struggle of balancing hurt feelings, but she usually only laughed and said she had him and that was enough. A small smile spread across his face. He'd pridefully earned his place at her side by never underestimating her and had selfishly been content being the only one there. Now, however, he was eager for her to broaden her circle of companions, to open her heart and life to more than just him.

"Jargon! You've finally caught up." Frawnden sighed in relief and waved him over. "Do you mind just waiting here? I need to go see if I can get a quiver of these new arrows. They're fletched with magic-enhanced *Ñáwag-gazu* feathers, and I don't want to be the only one shooting old arrows. I'll only be a moment!" Without a second glance back, she galloped off with the other Centaurs behind, their eyes glowing in adoration.

"Oh, yes, that's alright. Just abandon me as soon as I arrive. No worries about hard feelings at all." He rolled his eyes as he let his medical bag slide off his shoulder. With quick hands, he found the salve he needed, swiped a glob onto his finger, then spread it onto his blister. Instant relief flooded through him. With a few words in the Centaur language to ensure the magic in the salve was properly released, he watched with proud fascination as the swelling and color went down. In a few hours, it would be completely healed. The art and magic of medicine never ceased to amaze him.

Looking around, he found where the spectators were gathering around the roped-off archery range. Some of the range's targets were painted wooden circles; others were carved animals. All of them were already littered with arrows and holes as the archers rushed to complete their final warm-ups and practice shots.

A bugle horn sounded—the last five-minute warning. Knowing Frawnden would forget to come back before the competition's start, he moved from where she left him. Mingling with the rest of the spectators, he worked his way through them until he arrived at the front of the crowd, the rope barrier only inches away.

After only a few moments, his gaze tired of the arrows and bows, shifting instead to the grass below, searching for any thistles he could collect later for a new anxiety-soothing potion he was developing.

"Who are you here to see?" A voice accompanied by a tap on Jargon's hip startled him from his search.

"Oh, what's that?" He looked down to see a very young Centaur peering up at him with wide eyes. A thick strand of blonde hair fell into her eyes; the rest of her mane cascaded down her back in a long braid.

"Who are you here to see?" she repeated.

Squinting into the suns' bright noonday light,

he searched for Frawnden. As he'd predicted, she was already lining up at her mark, just three archers from where he stood on the sidelines. Bending to the young Centaur's height, he pointed. "Do you see the buckskin woman with the caramel skin and black hair?"

The young girl's eyes widened. "That's Frawnden."

"Very good."

The girl reared up and stamped her hooves. "Me too! I want to be just like her when I grow up." She pressed herself against the rope, looking as if she were going to gallop straight to Frawnden and throw herself upon her.

Jargon laughed and ruffled the girl's messy braid. "You know, she doesn't just do archery."

A frown dipped her golden brow as she looked back up at him. "She doesn't?"

Though a legend to the rest of Trans-Falls, to Jargon, Frawnden was still the little Centaur girl who had fallen down a small ravine and scrapped her knees, coming to him and his father for healing. Since that day, they'd become fast friends, hardly ever leaving each other's side. Frawnden also learned the magic of medicine then—her fiercest passion.

"She's also an excellent medic."

The girl's blue eyes shifted to his satchel and the medic symbol sewn onto it. "Like you?"

A broad grin swept his face as he nodded. "Just like me."

Then, before she could ask the next question that parted her lips, the last bugle sounded, and the competition began.

For a group of wild, boisterous creatures that the Trans-Falls Centaurs were, they remained impeccably quiet as the competing archers took their turns, only erupting into cheers when each Centaur finished shooting.

Without breaking a sweat and with no surprise to Jargon or any of the other onlookers, Frawnden shot a perfect score, her grouping in the center of the bullseye unmatched.

With the first half of the competition over, a small break commenced.

"Shall we get some water?" Jargon asked the young Centaur who hadn't left his side since their introduction.

"I prefer *muluk*." Then she stuck out her hand. "I'm Areena."

He gripped her forearm, night-black and

moon-white skin meeting. "I'm Jargon. May the suns smile upon your presence."

Her grin displayed a couple missing teeth—the carefree smile of a child. "As do the stars sing upon yours. I love your hair." Then taking his hand in hers, she trotted off to the refreshments, leaving him no choice but to hide his smile and try keep pace with an awkward gait somewhere between a fast walk and trot. Subconsciously, he touched his fingers to his hair. Frawnden had been the one to encourage him to grow his hair long and weave it into dreadlocks. She'd be pleased to hear someone else appreciated it.

Though Areena kept speaking to him, trying to get him to try the assortment of iced herbal *muluk* and juices available for the spectators, he couldn't keep his attention from roving across the heads of the other Centaurs. Sometimes being taller than average had its perks. But the Centaur he searched for had not yet arrived. *Most likely they'll announce him. The return of a chief and his son isn't taken lightly.*

When he'd satisfied Areena by accepting a rosemary and lemon *muluk* juice mix she'd made, they let the crowd sweep them back toward the range. They pushed their way back to the rope. As soon as he spotted five elite guards on the range, he knew his suspicions were correct.

"*Zuru fuñofufe*," he cursed. His glance landed on Frawnden, and by the way her arms crossed, and her brows furrowed in a scowl, he knew she was just as displeased as him, though for a very different reason.

Out of the woods a tall gray Centaur trotted, his son in tow. The blue markings on his body left no doubt—he was the chief of Trans-Falls.

Without an uttered word, every Centaur extended a front leg and bowed low, fists over their hearts. Even Areena, young as she was, knew better than to hesitate in her display of respect and loyalty. Jargon chewed on his lip as Frawnden remained standing for just a second longer than everyone else and stared defiantly at the Chief's son. Only after their eyes locked did she slowly kneel.

Stars be cursed, Frawnden. Are you trying to lose your chance at the elite archery guard? But he knew she didn't strive to simply be on the elite archery team; she wanted to be the best of them all. The only Centaur good enough at archery to threaten her chance at best Trans-Falls archer was the one standing before them—the next chief of Trans-Falls, Aeron.

"Rise, my people! Let these Warriors finish their proving, then let us celebrate by the

Gauyuyáwa and drink to their success!"

The ground shook as the Centaurs stood, shouting their welcomes and war cries and emphasizing them by striking their hooves into the soft dirt.

Just before Aeron took his place among the elite archers, he looked to Jargon, a grim shadow in his stony gray eyes. Jargon slowly shook his head, hoping Aeron would know what he meant. Then the bustling crowds and archers broke their gaze.

As each round proceeded, Jargon thought back to the conversation he'd unexpectedly had with Aeron mere days ago while collecting herbs near his cabin.

"I'm glad to see you followed your passion." A voice startled Jargon, and he quickly dropped his hooves from trying to reach a cluster of zheborgiy *mushrooms high on a tree trunk. Whirling around, he came face to face with someone he hadn't seen in over thirty years.*

Narrowing his eyes, he assessed the Centaur. Though he'd grown into a fine Centaur adult, he still looked very similar to how he'd looked all those years ago: gray speckled body, silver hair, and stone-colored eyes. "Glad to see you've finally returned to Trans-Falls, Aeron, chief-son." Jargon bowed but Aeron scoffed.

"Please don't. You know me better than that."

"Knew," Jargon corrected quietly. "Knew you better than that. It's been many years." His eyes met Aeron's again, searching for arrogance, for any ill reason for seeking him out privately in the woods. He found none ... yet.

"Yes." Aeron's eyes grew distant and misty. "My mother wished to be with her home tribe in her last years before the sickness took its toll."

"So she's gone."

"Indeed."

"I'm very sorry."

"As am I."

But Jargon was apologizing for more than just her death. Though he and his father had spent countless hours studying her and even finding evidence of the ancient Corrupt Magic, Kijaqumok *in her blood, they hadn't been able to stop it. Her death brought the end of their chance to discover its origins and find a cure should anyone else contract the dark magic. His fists tightened; somehow, he would have to find another way to study the* Kijaqumok. *Something in his heart told him it wasn't the last time they would fight against it.*

"Are they always so difficult to gather?"

Jargon frowned, unsure of what Aeron was asking

about until he pointed a finger at the mushrooms. "Oh. Yes, though usually more so. I'm lucky to have found this cluster so close to the ground. Usually, they grow higher, or else the Zelauw-fafu get to them."

Aeron nodded, eyes lingering unusually long on the mushrooms. "Are they important to you? To your healing, I mean?"

"Very."

"Actually, Jargon, I've come for a much different reason."

"Oh?" Though surprised by the turn of conversation, having thought Aeron came to accuse himself and his father for not saving his mother, Jargon couldn't help but step forward in intrigue. He hadn't missed the nervousness in Aeron's voice.

A blush raced across the chief-son's cheeks. "You're friends with the archer Frawnden, are you not?"

The black hair on Jargon's body stood up. "Why do you ask?"

Aeron blew out a heavy breath and scratched the back of his neck. "I was wondering if you could introduce us? I've admired her skill for years, and it was actually watching her before I left Trans-Falls that inspired me to take up archery myself."

The laugh in Jargon's chest started as a chuckle

then finished as a roar. "You fancy her? You'll have to wish on the stars for that one. She's already rejected everyone I've tried to match her with thus far. What makes you think you'll be any different?"

Aeron's shoulder slumped, and for the first time since he'd started playing matchmaker for Frawnden years ago, Jargon found himself pitying one of Frawnden's admirers.

He tried to soften the rejection with fact. "The legends of your own skill have traveled far. You are the only archer in Ravenwood who can beat her, and she hates you for it. I'm afraid you've not much a chance."

Aeron's eyes flashed with determination. "I'm not looking to best her. I'm looking to win her hand, and I'm prepared to lose at archery if I must."

Jargon's eyes widened. "No, that's not the right way to it. She'd know what you did the second you did it and would hate you all the more for it. She's come this far because of her hard work, not because others have let her win."

"Then what must I do?"

"You must shoot the same as you always have and leave the result up to fate. If you win, so be it, and if you lose, then it shone in the stars."

"There must be something you can do to help me, though. I've seen the way you two are together. You

know her better than anyone. Surely, she loves more than archery, something else I can find common ground on?"

Then a strange, horrible idea flickered to life in Jargon's mind. He hated himself for thinking it but knew it would be the only way Aeron could break the wall Frawnden had built out of her pride and ambition. But he couldn't tell Aeron what to do; the chief-son would have to be smart enough to think of it himself.

"I don't know why you're so enamored with her, or even if your heart is pure in intention, but I've studied the mind and subsequent personalities all my life. Nothing in your words, eyes, or body tells me you have wrong in your heart, and I doubt you're smart enough to lie on all those fronts. Which is why I'll give you one hint. Only one"

"Anything." Aeron's jaw set with determination.

"Archery may be her ambition, but medicine is her passion." Jargon turned away, a small grin on his lips. If anyone had a chance at Frawnden's heart, it was Aeron—of that, he was sure. "The rest is up to you."

Aeron stamped his hoof, a broad grin across his face. He clapped a hand to Jargon's shoulder, fire in his eyes. "Thank you so much."

Jargon shrugged. "Just don't tell her I helped you or even that we talked. She likes to be made to think it's her idea."

The chief-son nodded solemnly, drinking in every word as if it were the water of everlasting wisdom. "Of course. I'll find a way to make this up to you, though. I promise."

"Don't thank me yet."

"Jargon! Jargon!" Areena's high-pitched voice and gentle slaps against his side startled him from the memory. "The chief-son and Frawnden are the last competitors!"

Jargon's stomach flipped as his eyes landed on the gray and buckskin Centaurs standing next to each other, hooves on their marks. Aeron's eyes were soft and adoring as he gazed down at her; Frawnden's burned with determination. Down range, two hoops only just wide enough for an arrow to pass through hung from tree branches. The distance was staggering, the targets extremely small and hard to see. Most Centaurs would be happy to hit even near the target from that distance. Aeron and Frawnden would be shooting *through* the rings until one of them missed.

Jargon sent a silent prayer to the Great Emperor. He remembered how Aeron had been when they were both young, playing together while their parents spoke of battles against the Etas, the mess the Duvarharian traitor Thaddeus and his dragon were making of Ventronovia, and of the dark magic that had plagued Aeron's mother since a battle many years ago. All those years ago, Aeron had been kind and just, a lover of animals and of academic learning as much as he was of the sword. Jargon had seen no malicious spirit in him then and still saw none in him now. Side by side, he and Frawnden were stunning. If any Centaur deserved to lead the tribe of Trans-Falls alongside its chief, it was Frawnden.

But only if Aeron could win her heart.

With the trumpeting of a bugle, the final round commenced.

Frawnden stood motionless as a statue, one arm extended, holding the bow, the other bringing the fletched end of the arrow to her cheek. Her chests rose then fell, steady and measured each time until she held her breath and released the string.

The arrow whistled through the air. The ring swung gently on its string, the arrow lodged into the tree trunk behind it, perfectly in line with the hole.

"Have you ever seen something so incredible?" Areena's eyes remained unblinking on the rings in disbelief.

Jargon laughed nervously. "No. It's quite impressive."

"It's *impossible* at three-hundred-fifty feet."

Yet the impossible had been proven possible by Trans-Falls's most adored archer. Jargon's heart pounded with excitement and pride.

Other Warriors removed Frawnden's arrow from the tree and stilled the ring. The crowd turned to Aeron.

Ignoring Frawnden's challenging gaze, he calmly notched an arrow to his string and pulled it back, mimicking the same stance and stillness she'd maintained moments before.

After several deep breaths, he released the arrow. It followed a similar path to Frawnden's as it streaked through the ring and into the tree trunk behind it. The ring spun from being nicked by the arrow's feathers.

But instead of waiting for the ring and arrow to be reset, Frawnden took her stance again and rapidly released her second arrow.

The sound of splitting wood filled the air. The crowd gasped.

"Unbelievable," Jargon whispered. Her arrow had flown through the spinning ring, splitting

Aeron's behind it.

Elation brightened her face as the crowd roared with excitement and declaring her the winner. Even the judges moved forward, ready to make the announcement and end the games.

But Aeron notched another arrow. The crowd gasped.

"What will he do? He can't possibly outdo that!" Areena gripped Jargon's leg fiercely as his eyes narrowed.

"He can't. She shot the best of the round. Even if he repeated the shot, he'd still come in second because she did it first." *What are you planning, chief-son?*

The world slowed as Aeron pulled back his string. Immediately, Jargon knew something was off. Aeron's stance shifted, his aim no longer on the ring. But if he wasn't aiming at it ... then what *was* he aiming for?

With an abrupt yelp, Aeron stamped his hoof, flinched, and released the string.

The arrow sang through the air. It flew past the ring and disappeared into the branches. A moment later, a crash echoed in the forest.

The crowd fell silent, then hummed with wondering whispers. Had Aeron shot an animal? Perhaps he'd missed because his frustration clouded him.

But despite the confusion, the victor was clear. The judges declared Frawnden the unchallenged winner of the elite games, and Trans-Falls' best archer. The crowd surged forward onto the range.

"What happened?" Areena's frustrated gaze searched for answers as she reared back on two legs, trying to see over and through the cheering crowd. Her hand held relentlessly onto Jargon's to keep them from being separated.

Jargon shook his head as he pushed his way to where Frawnden, Aeron, and the other three winners were being declared members of the Igentis' team of elite archers.

Tears gathered in Frawnden's face as she accepted the flower wreath upon her head then congratulated her competitors. The fire of jealousy she'd looked at Aeron with faded into relief and respect.

"I almost thought you'd top my last shot." A nervous laugh rang from her lips as she shook her head.

Aeron shrugged. "How could I have? Yours was the best."

One of the other finalists asked the question on everyone's mind: "Then why did you shoot again?"

The onlookers fell silent, waiting for the answer.

Rubbing the back of his neck, Aeron laughed. "Desperation, I suppose. But the Great Emperor humbled me. A bug bit my ankle and ruined the shot. The win was yours, Frawnden—it shone in the stars."

Though the audience was satisfied, Jargon saw no evidence of such a bite on Aeron's ankle. *He wasn't aiming at the rings to begin with. What is he planning?*

Areena's voice snapped him from his thoughts. "Of course, she won; she's the best. Are you proud of her?" She ducked behind him, nervously sneaking peeks at the winners.

Jargon laughed. "Yes. Very much so."

Nodding solemnly, Areena announced she was going back to drink more *muluk* and juice before it ran out. Jargon watched with amusement as she trotted off, disappearing into the crowd.

Then Frawnden's eyes landed on Jargon. A huge grin lit up her face as she rushed to him and threw her arms around his neck. "I made it!"

Jargon laughed as he returned her embrace. "I'm so happy for you, Frawnden. You deserve it and more."

Giving him an extra hard squeeze, she let out a long sigh. "Thank you, Jargon. I couldn't have done it without your support."

He winked as she drew away. "Oh, I think you could've."

"Well, maybe." She flicked her mane off her shoulders and smirked.

"Frawnden! We're going to the falls to celebrate. Are you coming?" One of the victors already had a bottle of wine in his hand.

"Of course! But I want to see what Aeron's last shot fell. The crash was quite loud, and if it's an animal, I want to make sure it's not suffering."

Aeron nodded solemnly. "Good idea. I'll come along. We'll meet up at the falls later."

Frawnden gestured for Jargon and Aeron to follow as they made their way to the tree the ring hung from. Jargon made sure to keep respectful distance between him and Aeron. He didn't want Frawnden thinking they'd met previously or that Jargon had anything to do with the competition's unusual ending.

"Oh! A cluster of *zheborgiy!*" Frawnden cantered to the mushrooms. Dropping her bow, she scooped the fungus into her arms. the cluster nearly as large as her head—an extremely rare find. "How fortunate!" She tilted her head back, searching the trees, and Jargon followed her gaze. Clusters that size only grew extremely high up—usually an impossible height for Centaurs to reach.

"Very fortunate indeed," Jargon muttered. When his gaze met Aeron's, he knew this had been his plan all along. Jargon hid his smile.

"Are those useful?" The confusion on Aeron's face didn't waver. If Jargon hadn't told him the importance of the *zheborgiy* fungus just days before, he could've believed Aeron had no idea what treasure Frawnden held.

Frawnden scoffed as she examined the fungus cluster. All barriers around her heart shattered under the force of her passion. She stamped her hooves in excitement, her tail swishing from side to side. "For medicine you mean? You have no idea."

A victorious grin spread across Aeron's face as his eyes softened with admiration. "Then give me an idea."

Her eyebrows shot up. Clearly, she'd never

considered the chief-son would be interested in medicine. "You really want to know?"

"Of course." Aeron bowed slightly. "It is my duty as the heir of Trans-Falls to learn all I can about the lives and responsibilities of my people. Medicine is essential to the wellbeing of the tribe, and I think it's past time I learn more about it."

Jargon had never seen her more eager to share her passion. In only moments, she was drowning Aeron in seemingly endless medical terms, spells, plants, and magic types. The corners of Jargon's lips twitched in a grin as Aeron glanced back at him, expression full of gratitude.

Though Jargon couldn't guarantee Aeron would win over the wildness of Frawnden's heart, at least he had the chance to try. Of all the Centaurs Jargon had sent her way, he hoped and prayed for Aeron's success the most.

Turning, he quietly took his leave, hooves striking loudly against the stone path through the dense forest. He was only mildly surprised when a young, blonde-haired, golden-bodied Centaur joined him, both hands full of *muluk* and juice.

"What do you want to do when you grow up, Jargon?"

Though he laughed, he didn't try to correct her

by saying he already *was* grown up. Instead, he stroked his goatee and pondered her words. His father had been the *Uwarñoe*, the Head Medic, of Trans-Falls for years, but that title wasn't passed from father to son like Chief; it had to be earned. Though he loved medicine, he hadn't aspired to any particular position, other than to be the best medic he personally could be. But what if he tried for more?

"I don't know. Maybe *Uwarñoe.* That's what they call the Head Medic of Trans-Falls."

She drank the rest of one drink before stacking the empty cup under her other. Then she threaded her fingers through his and smiled. "Do you think you'll be chosen?"

He thought of Aeron and Frawnden, of the excitement they'd shared, and all their similarities they were soon to discover. He also remembered how Aeron promised to return the favor of giving him a chance with Frawnden. His tail swished in hopeful anticipation as he chuckled. "I don't know, but I think I'll have a better chance than most."

GROUNDED TOGETHER

Cavos Hatching Grounds
Ruins of Yazkuza, Cavos Desert
Year: Rumi 189 Q.RJ.M

THOUGH VERENA DIDN'T MANAGE the largest dragon hatching grounds, she certainly felt she managed the busiest, especially during the hatching and bonding season.

"Hey!" Waving, Verena jogged toward a dragon who was struggling to lift an egg onto a cart. Nearly twice the size of the dragon's head, the polished eggshell didn't fit well in the dragon's sharp claws. The egg tottered and swayed on the edge of the cart as the dragon beat her small wings harder, planting horrific images of a cracked shell into Verena's mind. "Hey! What in Susahu did I say about lifting eggs bigger than your head? Put it down and let a bigger dragon do it."

A flush of red spread through the white dragon's scales as she lowered the egg back to the sand; the egg slipped from her grasp and dropped the last few inches with a dull *thud.* Sand swirled in the air as she landed and meekly folded her wings, slinking to the side as Verena quickly checked the egg for any damage. Besides a few unsightly scratches, no lasting harm had been done.

With the rag she kept tucked in her belt, Verena polished away a smudge until she stared into her own reflection, eyes the same blue green as the egg's shell. Briefly, she wondered if her own dragon had sired this clutch.

It's hard to tell. There were so many sweet dragons in mating season. How could I have picked just one? Her dragon's deep voice echoed in her mind. She narrowed her eyes and stood, brushing sand from her breeches.

Davian, I swear you're a bit of a klushuuv sub.

You would be too if you were as beautiful as I.

I'm beautiful too.

Only because you're bonded to me.

Verena couldn't argue. Before she'd bonded with Davian, her hair had been lackluster brown to match her eyes. After bonding with him, her hair and eyes turned the same green and blue gradient as his scales.

Although, you are quite a heartbreaker. I'd say your actions are worse than mine. At least the dragons I dote upon have a good time to remember. The riders you've turned away only have bitter rejection.

I'm proud to prefer enjoying my bed alone.

As you should be.

Are you going to keep sunning yourself, or shall you come move your clutch properly since you're the only dragon here big enough to do it?

Is that a compliment?

It's an insult to your enormous ego. Get down here.

Hands on her hips, Verena peered into the double glaring suns and wondered what purpose it served Hanluurasa, the sky realm, to have two of them when one seemed bright enough. Using her hand to shield her eyes, she watched her dragon stretch lethargically on his perch at the top of the high arena-like walls encircling the incubation confinement. With a push off the rock, he gracefully glided to the hot sand. When he landed, the rocks hardly shook despite his massive size, the wind only stirring with a whisper as if his wings were a pleasant disruption. Pride filled her as she watched him slink closer, his lithe body slithering across the hot sand, as much a part of the world and sky as he was himself. It never ceased to amaze her how even Rasa seemed mesmerized by his powers.

It's the same around you. You're just too stubborn to see it.

One of us has to keep a level head.

I'm sure glad it's you. It's so much more fun to simply be beautiful.

Effortlessly, he reached for the egg and wrapped one set of claws around it, hoisting it into the cart and leaning it against the numerous cushions. Jumping up next to it, Verena made quick work of the ropes to secure it. With the cart now full, she tapped her hand to the *Fuse*—a large buffalo-like pack animal—sending her intentions into its mind. With a low bellow, the *Fuse* nudged its partner, and in sync, they pulled. The cart lurched once before starting its journey to the large gate, their pace excruciatingly slow.

The trek from incubation confinement to bonding arena was short. If she wanted, she could have dragons fly the eggs over the walls, but Verena never took chances with the eggs. She'd seen the mistakes other hatching grounds had made, and she wasn't in any position to make those same ones. The bonding of dragons and riders should never be taken lightly.

When she turned her attention back to the two dragons, she rolled her eyes.

The little white female pranced in front of Davian like a fool, blushing fiercely. Davian looked down at her, nearly twice her size, a sparkle of amusement in his eyes.

Knock it off.

I'm not doing anything, he insisted. But the wavering green and blue shimmer around him dulled slightly, and with it, the small dragon's blush.

"You!" Verena pointed an accusatory finger toward the Cloud Dragon. "The next cart is coming in. Load it with eggs and, by the stars, don't pick up the ones bigger than your head. Understand?"

The dragon nodded quickly and purred, taking one last long glance back at Davian before scampering off to a clutch of small red eggs.

She was just telling me what a handsome rider she has. Coincidentally, he's about your age.

Don't care.

Unfortunately.

With years of practiced ease, Verena climbed up Davian's leg. Most riders rode at the base of their dragon's necks, just in front of the shoulders, but Davian had grown to a size that made riding there uncomfortable. She'd been forced to move just behind his head, nestled between two protruding spines. Over time, the spines and scales had molded to the shape of her body—a fine example of how a rider and dragon's soul bond changed them physically, not just mentally. Now she didn't have to use a saddle; she pitied any rider still forced to use one.

"Let's get to the bonding arena. I want to make sure your clutch arrives safely. They're going to draw in quite the crowd once the news of Seduction Dragons takes flight."

Aren't you proud of me for bringing back a nearly extinct dragon kind?

Though she groaned and rolled her eyes, she truly was extremely proud. It seemed unlikely that a Kind like the Seduction Dragon could come close to extinction, but their ability to seduce even Rasa itself had proved to be their downfall. Seduction wasn't limited to procreation; it'd also been exploited for deception and manipulation.

About two hundred years ago, before the rise of the Great Lord and the start of the Duvarharian and Ventronovian Golden Age, Davian's kind had been made illegal and nearly hunted to extinction. Now under the Great Lord's laws of acceptance and freedom, Davian had been free to live, bond, and procreate. For that, Verena was very thankful.

Though Verena was a shrewd businessperson and hard worker, she had to attribute some of her hatching ground's success to her dragon's unique magic.

Already they were descending, having just crossed over the large wall dividing the two arenas. From the sky, the entire hatching ground site looked something like a honeycomb: each incubation zone and bonding arena fitted perfectly together, not a foot of space wasted. Her hatching ground wasn't the only like it. Myths spoke of a cross between an Insect and Stone Dragon who'd invented the design and built hundreds of them across the old ruins of Yazkuza, forming what collectively became known as the Cavos Hatching Grounds. Verena tended to believe the myths because none of the honeycomb arenas had been chiseled or shaped by tool. It appeared as if the designs had grown from the desert spires on their own.

She and Davian landed in a secluded corner of the bonding arena where they wouldn't draw too much attention. The hatchings were already in full swing—the sand littered with broken eggshells, the air filled with the cries of hatchlings and excited riders, all searching for their soulmates. A few maintenance dragons and riders raced across the sand, attempting to clean it and keep the space open for more eggs. Between the jumping, screeching hatchlings and the embryotic fluid clinging to boots and claws in a sandy, sticky mess, the workers had their hands and claws full.

Verena thanked the Great Lord she wasn't one of them anymore.

She was also grateful to longer be an announcer. That'd been the job she despised most when climbing the hatching ground's ranks. Her eyes lingered on the orange-yellow-haired rider astride his shining Sun-Flash Dragon. Each time the dragon shook her feathery mane, rays of sunlight scattered throughout the arena, drawing attention back to itself. The light display distracted the crowds just enough to keep them focused on the announcements stating when they could enter the arena or when ordered behind the stone barrier as a new clutch was brought forth.

I miss that position. I never understood why you didn't like it. They loved us. They couldn't take their eyes off us.

That was the problem, Verena laughed as she remembered the swooning crowds. *It's the announc-*

er's job to re-direct attention, not completely steal it.

Same thing.

Not even a little.

Verena shot a nearby dragon a nasty scowl when they pranced a little too close to her and Davian. With a whimper, the dragon scurried away, their rider just as embarrassed to be caught staring.

The announcers moved to Verena and Davian's side of the arena and gestured to the clutch of blue and green eggs, stating their origin: a mix between Seduction Dragon and Rainbow Dragon.

Oh, yes, I remember her. Davian ruffled his wings, and an unwanted volley of memories cascaded through Verena's mind. Immediately, she blocked them and shook her head to clear the images from her thoughts.

Oh, Verena, don't be such a child. Mating is a beautiful and natural thing.

Doesn't make me any more interested in it. Besides, those are your private memories. I don't have any desire to be a part of them.

Suit yourself. He shrugged, but she could hear the amusement in his thoughts.

Despite her lack of interest in exactly how

the clutch had been made, the combination of a Rainbow and Seduction Dragon was beautiful and extremely rare. She had no doubt the hatchlings would grow to be an inspiration to the Cavos Hatching Grounds, and hopefully beyond. The arena roared to life with excitement when the announcer stated this clutch was one of two Seduction Dragon clutches ready to hatch today.

Verena's heart swelled as the announcer waved his hand and three openings appeared in the stone wall to let the riders through. The vast majority of the riders were under the age of thirty. Knowing the Seduction Dragons would likely be bonded with the younger generation comforted her. Duvarharia needed new blood to take hold of the lost magic and kinds.

The sound of cracking shells filled the arena, quickly followed by the cries of hatchlings struggling to free themselves into the world. In just a few minutes, the arena filled with hatchlings testing their new wings and legs, some of them quiet and timid, others knocking down other hatchlings and riders. The hatchings proceeded quickly, and in less than an hour, all the Seduction and Rainbow hatchlings had been bonded with riders and ushered into an adjacent arena to be cleaned and given basic counseling on living with and caring for their new soulmate.

Are you crying?

Verena quickly brushed the tears from her cheeks. “No,” she grumbled. But as much as she denied it, she couldn’t help but be moved by the beauty and chaos of hatching day. The love shared between the soul of a dragon and rider was like no other. She was eternally grateful to not only have been born in an era when bonding was accessible for every Duvarharian but also to be able to play such a huge role in the hatchings and bondings.

Since she’d taken over this particular hatching grounds, the bonding rate had risen from sixty percent of dragons bonded to almost ninety-five percent. But that had nothing to do with her or her dragon’s unique magic. It had everything to do with them abolishing any rules about entrance and bonding fees or licenses, class restrictions, and all mating restrictions, rules, or fees. Anyone was free to come to their hatching grounds and try their fate at finding their soulmate.

They even allowed mother dragons to incubate the eggs themselves if they wished. Some of them were present even now, watching from the top of the arena walls as their clutches safely hatched and bonded.

Now whether or not the newly bonded riders wanted to buy saddles, scale brushes, claw files, or other dragon accessories ... well, the hatching grounds had to make its money somehow.

Verena had worked tirelessly for years to achieve this success: a freedom where every dragon and rider was accepted and allowed their chance to find a soulmate. She wanted that to never change.

WHAT A SUCCESS. *You should be very proud of yourself.*

Verena grinned as the familiar old voice reverberated in her mind. Looking up, she found herself gazing upside down into a graying Combustion Dragon's face.

"It is and I am."

With a pained growl, the old dragon climbed down the arena wall and dropped to the ground. Though she'd seen it many times, her eyes strayed to the stump on his shoulder where one of his wings had once grown but was now missing.

He'd always insisted she address it rather than stare and ignore, so she asked, "How's your shoulder? Hurting anymore since we got those

Centaur salves imported for you?"

Another low groan rumbled from his throat as he looked back at his shoulder, milky eyes blinking slowly in the suns. She wondered how well he could see these days.

As good as it can be. The salves have helped immensely, but I'm afraid nothing can help my damaged pride. Never did like anything lopsided.

I think you look absolutely stunning, Davian purred as he peered up and down the Combustion Dragon's one fiery red scales, now speckled with gray.

I'm not sure I can believe a dragon like you, Davian. Don't you flatter everyone?

No, Davian answered flatly as he licked his claws. *I have no problem pointing out flaws and unattractiveness. If it weren't for Verena's adorable, charming personality, she would've been far too ugly for me to bond with.*

Verena smacked the top of his head but couldn't help but laugh. Growing up plain and uninteresting in looks had forced her to develop something of a shrewd personality and thick skin. Although, being bonded to a Seduction Dragon meant she turned away more suitors than she had ever wanted to be bothered with.

But I mean it. Truly. The gray speckles in your scales are such a delightful gradient. I love how they sparkle in the moonlight like little stars. Most dragons gray from head to tail in one boring shade, but you, Bjartur, have truly mastered the art of aging. Any rider or dragon would be proud to bond or mate with you.

Though his words were sincere and meant to cheer the old dragon, they only made his shoulder sag. *If only that were true, beautiful dragon. But I fear my chance for mating or even for bonding are long behind me.*

With a sad smile, Verena reached out to touch Bjartur's cheek. He leaned into her small touch, her hand dwarfed by a massive eye even bigger than Davian's.

"Don't give up hope just yet. The day is not yet over, and there are still many riders looking for a soulmate. You never know what the Creator has in mind."

To his credit, Bjartur curled his lips over his fangs in something like a smile and nodded. "*Of that you are right. Perhaps there is still hope for me. If you find a rider who likes to play lots of kinuneb and doesn't care to fly, let me know.*" The bitterness in his words pierced Verena's heart as he turned to climb back up the wall, grunts of exertion and pain echoing off the stone.

"I will," Verena promised. She watched him go before turning back to the bonding arena, continuing her long day of supervision.

She believed her own words; there *was* still hope. But as the suns continued to sink toward the horizon and the number of hours until closing grew smaller, not a single rider paid any attention to the lonely old dragon perched high on the walls above them.

CAN YOU IMAGINE *how hard it would be to fight in the last greatest war of your time and to finally eradicate the last of the creatures who had been plaguing your people for millennia, only to lose your rider and a wing, and then be ostracized by the very people you saved simply because your country's very infrastructure doesn't accommodate disabilities?*

I can't imagine. I honestly don't know how Bjartur goes on each day. Especially two hundred years after losing his rider. Any other dragon would've gone mad by now.

He's not any other dragon.

Verena's thoughts shifted to the wise Combustion Dragon. He and his rider had been the leaders of a Wing—a battalion of a hundred riders and dragons—in the last war against the Etas. They'd been at the front of the final charge, in the middle of the worst danger and bloodshed. It was nothing short of a miracle Bjartur hadn't lost his life alongside his rider. Only a very strong dragon could continue fighting the way he had, live through the horrors he had, and come out alive and mostly whole.

Perhaps he has more hope for himself than we give him credit for.

Verena looked up to where Bjartur still sat in the setting suns, trying to soak up the last of the rays. The warmth always somewhat eased the aches in his bones.

Perhaps so. I only pray his hope has a happy ending.

I do as well.

A deep silence stretched between them as they walked beside each other, shattered eggshells crunching under their feet. Only a couple hatchlings were left in the arena along with a small crowd. One finally bonded with a rider, but the other three wandered off, their soulmate not among the remaining crowd. If they didn't find a soulmate tomorrow, Verena would help move them to another hatching ground where they could appeal to a different crowd. Because the number of riders usually outnumbered the dragons—especially since many dragon kinds had been hunted or outlawed not long ago—it usually fell to the dragon to pick the rider, even if the final bond was consensual. While most dragons quickly found a rider to pick, some grew past the typical bonding period without a rider. Their chances of bonding after that slimmed as their natural bonding instincts gave way to more calculated and logic-driven choices. The beauty of bonding was usually the attraction of one soul calling to another despite all logic; the more thought applied, the less likely a pair was to bond. But if a bonding *did* happen between an older rider and dragon, with both logically choosing the other while also following the calling of their souls, the bond would always be stronger.

Verena placed her hand on Davian's leg as they walked across the sand, drawing curious and desiring glances as they subconsciously encouraged the remaining crowd to make their way toward the gates. She'd bonded with Davian at the considerably young age of forty, just after graduating from a prestigious academy dedicated to the study of all dragon kinds. Constructed in the Cavos Hatching Grounds by order of the first Great Lord, the academy strove to abolish old stigmas around hatchings and dragon kinds. Since she'd been born to a family of little wealth, she'd had to work multiple jobs to pay for the schooling, which caused her to graduate twice as slow as the others. But watching the younger riders try to wrestle large dragons and eggs with immature magic and experience didn't make her envy them one bit.

By the time she'd found her way to a hatching ground to seek her own soulmate, most hatchlings considered her too old to bond with. Discouraged, she'd wandered through the old ruins of Yazkuza, the ancient dragon city, and stumbled upon a gathering of once shunned dragon kinds. There she'd met Davian, her soul inexplicably drawn to his. But being nearly sixty years old, Davian had hesitated, having to think the bond through rather than simply follow his soul. In the end, they chose each other willingly. The bond formed between them had felt like fire, and as soon as it had formed, she knew it was like no other. They were tied inexplicably to each other. For every moment after that, despite their differences, they had been one creature.

She wanted that kind of bond for all the hatchlings born under her care and for every rider who came through their gates. But more than anything, she wanted that for Bjartur.

"Excuse me?" a very timid voice called from somewhere on the other side of Davian.

They paused their walk to address the guest.

The young girl, likely only a few years from adulthood, stood just by the gate, eyes darting out to the long stairs, then back into the arena. Disappointment shone in her misty eyes, but Verena sensed hope within her.

"What can I help you with?"

When the girl met Verena's eyes, she blushed fiercely and stuttered, "I–I was w–wondering if I'd have another ch–chance tomorrow?"

A warm smile lifted Verena's cheeks as she stretched out her hand to guide the girl past the gates. "Of course. We have about twenty more clutches, which gives us at least another two days of hatching. Then we should have another mass hatching in about six months. You're always welcome back. And if you ever care to volunteer, we could always use more eyes on the eggs."

Sniffing and dashing any remnants of discouragement from her eyes, she nodded quickly. "Thank you very much. I'll be back!" She dashed toward the steps in a flurry, and Verena feared for a moment she would fall. "May the suns smile upon your presence!" she called back before descending the stairs.

Verena laughed and whispered softly, knowing the girl was too far away to hear. "As do the stars sing upon yours."

You were just like that when we met, Davian grumbled low.

I was not.

Were too. You were spry and eager, although maybe a little bit more annoying.

Verena scoffed as she shielded her eyes against the setting suns.

You've grown quieter since those days.

Sixty years and a lot of responsibility will do that to you.

One hundred years is hardly old for a Duvarharian. And besides, I thought being around hatchlings and young riders was supposed to make you younger.

Tell that to my aching back and bones.

They fell into shared laughter as Verena stepped out to the impossibly long stairs, watching the crowds slowly make their way back to the sandy city below. The world of dragons to the dragon-less rider was a nearly impossible expanse to traverse. The same went for the flightless dragon. A heavy sigh escaped her lips.

The last rays of the suns' light made looming silhouettes out of the tall red desert spires climbing from the golden sand and rising to meet the walls of the canyon the Cavos Hatching Grounds sat in. Sometimes, Verena couldn't believe how old many of the stone-carved buildings were, some of them having been constructed thousands of years ago as the great dragon city of Yazkuza. Other times, when a step crumbled out from under her, she could believe it just fine.

As the land fell under darkness, they turned back to the gate. But before they could step through and lock it, a loud bell rang.

Verena paused, confused as she tried to place why the bell sounded so familiar.

The supply lift.

Verena frowned; her confusion only deepened. *Supplies are never delivered after noon. And I didn't order any special deliveries.*

Wishing she at least had a dagger on her, Verena circled around the outside wall of the arenas, a mere fifty feet of walking space between the walls and the cliff edge.

In the growing darkness, she could just barely see the giant gears and chains of the supply lift they used for deliveries that arrived on carts rather than delivery dragons. Something sat upon it. Something with wheels.

Scowling, she felt the hair bristle on her arms as Davian growled low.

Then the object *moved.*

Verena yelped and took two steps back in surprise before rushing forward. Davian's roar of warning echoed on the canyon walls.

"Wait! Don't attack! I'm not here to harm."

Verena's mind fell blank with confusion. She didn't see a person standing there. "Who are you? *What* are you?"

With a creak and a grunt, the object wheeled from the lift onto the stone cliff and into a shrinking ray of light.

Verena hadn't known what she'd expected, but it certainly hadn't been ... *that.*

The object was a chair with wheels: two big, two small. A rider sat upon it, hands poised over the two large wheels. A small stream of magic poured from his palms to the wheels, propelling the chair.

Verena's face must've shone with all her surprise and confusion because the rider laughed and apologized, "I'm so sorry to startle you. I didn't mean to be hiding in the shadows. I understand your confusion, but I'm afraid this is the only way I'm able to get around easily. Unfortunately, the stairs weren't an option."

Embarrassment at her initial shock flooded Verena as she surveyed the rider and realized what he meant. While his right foot rested on a small platform, the space where his left leg should've been was empty.

"Oh. Stars." Her face flushed, and she suddenly snapped her gaze anywhere but his missing leg or his eyes.

Davian stretched out his head, bringing his large eye close to the rider. Verena listened as he projected his thoughts into the rider's mind, grateful he spoke instead of her. *What brings you to our hatching grounds, little one?*

The rider's face mirrored Verena's as he blushed. "Well, I was hoping I could ... have a chance to ..." He didn't seem able to finish.

"Oh. Well, we're just about to close the gates tonight. Perhaps you could come back ..." She let her words trail off as her gaze roved back over the wheeled chair, then to the lift, then to his eyes, which dropped with embarrassed disappointment.

"I understand, but maybe I could stay the night? It was terribly difficult to convince the lift managers to let me ride up, and I'd hate to be late tomorrow as well."

Verena started and stopped several sentences. Their policy was very clear against guests staying the night. Gates opened at noon, and that was that. No one was even allowed onto the cliff ledge before then.

Davian tapped her back with his tail and gave her a look that spoke more than his thoughts ever could.

Clearing her throat, she straightened her shoulders and nodded curtly. "We don't usually allow guests to stay"—his shoulders dropped even farther—"but this is certainly a different situation entirely. Please, join us."

The excitement and gratitude that lit up his face washed all doubt from her heart.

With a flick of his hands, he compelled his white magic to propel the wheels, drawing beside Verena as they turned back to the gates.

Deeply interested in this rider who had gone so far out of his way to arrive at her hatching grounds, Verena couldn't help but sneak little glances at him. She guessed that if he stood, he'd be about her height, but there ended their similarities. Where her skin was dark and rich from long hours spent in the sun, his was ghostly white, as if he spent most of his time indoors. Unlike the average Duvarharian in the Cavos Desert who had dark hair to match their tanned complexion, his was blonde and fair. His characteristics were undoubtably northern Duvarharian. Judging by his gold jewelry and colorful clothes, she guessed he'd specifically hailed from Duvarharia's capital, the Dragon Palace.

Then what is he doing here?

Ask him.

That seemed much harder to do than weigh him and his story silently.

If you're to be our guest tonight, then we would like to exchange names. I am Davian, a Seduction Dragon, and this anti-social, awkward rider is my soulmate, Verena, the head manager of this hatching ground.

Verena scowled at her dragon, but he only winked.

The rider smiled and nodded his head in greeting. "Very lovely to meet you both. I'm Othello, son of Ellish, rider of Ryker, of the Council of the Dragon Palace."

Verena's eyebrows shot up. *He's practically*

royalty!

Davian licked his lips; a shimmer of his gentle magic settled around them and painted the world in vibrant colors. *How delightful.*

"What are you doing here?" The words tumbled from Verena's lips before she could refine them. For a moment, she wondered if Davian was right about her needing to work on her lackluster social skills.

But Othello didn't seem to mind; his eyes darted around the arena, taking in every inch of it while Verena locked the gate and cast a sealing spell on it. Though she still avoided his gaze, she listened with rapt attention to his response.

"I'm following the deepest, most innate desire of all Duvarharians—obtaining my soulmate." Some of the excitement in his eyes dulled with memory. "I've spent the last ten years visiting every hatching ground in the Dragon Palace and surrounding cities." He shook his head. "But you'd be surprised to find most hatchlings don't want a rider who can't fly with them."

Unfortunately, Verena wasn't surprised at all. Every young hatchling-rider dreamed of flying. One being forced to leave the other behind would be a tragedy akin to one of them dying. Most hatchlings wouldn't risk the heartbreak.

She pointed to his leg and the magic swirling around the wheels. "Why don't you just, you know, heal your leg with magic? Surely your father, as a Council member, could find a healer who—" Davian's tail smacked the back of Verena's head with considerable force, causing white stars to spot her vision. "What the—"

You just couldn't be more insensitive, could you?

That really hurt.

Heal it with magic, then, weakling.

Verena grumbled and rubbed the back of her head. Guilt swirled in her chest. Davian was right. She had no doubt that if magic could fix it, Othello wouldn't be here in a chair, having waited an entire day just to bypass the stairs.

"I'm very sorry." She swallowed her pride, leaving room for the apology on her lips. "That was extremely rude of me."

Othello lifted his chin, and despite the hurt in his eyes, he smiled. "I accept your apology. Unfortunately, magic cannot fix this for me, but I do not seek to fix it. I was born this way, and I believe this is how I was fashioned to be. It's held its hardships, but this is who I am and to expect magic to fix it would feel like a betrayal to myself. If that makes sense?"

Verena nodded slowly, not sure she understood at all but aware she'd never truly understand his predicament unless she herself experienced it. Taking a deep breath, she tried to release her expectations. Every rider had the freedom to live their life as they saw fit. If Othello had found peace in who he was, that was more than she'd had when his age.

"I deeply appreciate you accommodating me for the night. I promise I'll be a delightful guest and will stay only as long as the hatchings tomorrow. Then I'll be out of your scales."

Davian nudged Verena and nodded to the next arena where the last three hatchlings were being tended to by the care givers. *Perhaps he does not have to wait.*

A small smile lifted Verena's cheeks. "Actually, we have three hatchlings who've yet to bond. Would you like to meet them now?"

She didn't miss how his fists tightened and eyes flashed with uncertainty. But his voice was steady as he nodded and answered, "I would like that very much."

THREE QUICK GLANCES.

Three quick rejections.

Verena felt the disappointment radiate off Othello like the burning suns. She wanted to reach out, to place a hand on his shoulder, to reassure him that his chance wasn't over. But just like with any other rider, she couldn't guarantee a bonding, only a chance to try. Had his chances really run out?

I'm so sorry, little one. Davian enveloped Othello with his comforting magic and pressed his large snout to the young rider's chest.

Othello opened his mouth as if to whisper something then closed it. Instead of speaking, he wrapped his arms as far across Davian's snout as he could and wept.

Verena's heart ached with the sound. Her own tears sparkled in her eyes. Knowing she had no words to bridge such gaping sorrow, she laid a hand on his shoulder and poured all her sympathy into her touch and waited.

When his tears slowed, she whispered a question she'd wanted to ask since he rolled off the lift onto the stone spire. "Why here?"

Sniffing, he lifted his eyes to meet hers, his pale features strange in the flickering bonfire light. "I've heard so much about your hatching grounds. How you've opened them to anyone, how you have no regulations on who can bond or why. Your bonding rate is so much higher than the others in Duvarharia and even in the Cavos Desert. I thought maybe, if anywhere could give me a better chance ..." Bitterness lined his words.

She sank to her knees and folded her hands in her lap. Tears dropped from her eyes to the sand. "So we were your last hope."

The aching silence was answer enough.

Do not give up hope, little one. Davian whimpered in the way he did only when particularly upset. His magic's power was in making others feel good; when his magic wasn't enough to cheer someone up or make the world shine, his heart shattered right along with theirs. *There's always tomorrow. We have more eggs. You might—*

Othello looked up, a strange, sad peace in his eyes. "No. That's alright. I think—" He wiped his eyes and laughed, though the sound held no joy. "I think maybe it wasn't meant to be. I need to find peace in that. Maybe I have a purpose somewhere else."

But purpose aside, no rider was meant to be without a dragon, and no dragon without their rider. Nothing could change that.

"Othello—"

He cut her off by reaching for her hand, his eyes suddenly so much older than her own though he was a fraction of her age. "I suppose I'll just have to go home and be content playing *kinuneb*."

The name struck a memory in Verena. "Stars of all!" She jumped to her feet, startling Davian and Othello.

"What? I'm sorry if—"

"No, no!" She laughed, turning to Davian. Their thoughts mingled, and he roared in excitement, taking to the skies.

"Where is he going?" Othello's eyes shone with confusion and a touch of fear.

New tears of anticipation and excitement sparkled in Verena's eyes. "I have someone I want you to meet."

"BY THE GREAT LORD," Othello whispered, jaw dropping open. His eyes sparkled with the red of Bjartur's glowing scales.

Verena nodded and waved for Bjartur to come

closer. Though a few of his joints popped as he slunk across the sand, for the first time in years, he didn't complain about it. A strange look sparkled in his eyes.

"Othello, meet Bjartur."

They needed no other introduction. Hand on Davian's leg, Verena watched through misty eyes as Othello wheeled his chair through the sand until he sat mere inches from Bjartur's massive face.

"Your wing," Othello whispered as he looked to the stump where the dragon's right wing had once been.

Verena heard Bjartur's thoughts like a whisper on the wind as he projected them into Othello's mind. *And your leg.*

All at once, years of shared hardship, sorrow, loss, and loneliness were understood and validated. No longer were either of them alone in a world that catered only to the whole and bonded.

Bjartur's voice faded as his thoughts focused only on Othello's. In a similar fashion, Othello's voice dropped to a whisper.

It's beautiful.

Verena nodded, not bothering to hide her tears from Davian this time. She'd seen thousands of bondings, but none of them had felt so powerful as the one happening before her now. This wasn't a bonding made from blind instinct and attraction. This was a bonding that transcended time and space—one chosen not by logic, but by love, compassion, empathy, and understanding.

She caught the wispy end of their conversation.

I cannot carry you through the sky with me. We will always be destined to walk or climb. We will always be grounded.

Othello smiled brightly through the tears falling down his cheeks. "All my searching has brought me here, to this hatching ground, not so I could find another creature like me, but because our souls were meant to be, no matter what shape our bodies have taken. If I am to walk the earth like every other beast, then let it be for an eternity with you."

Huge dragon tears slipped from Bjartur's cloudy eyes as he bridged the gap between Othello's hand and his scales. *I choose you.*

And I, you.

Verena stuck two fingers between her lips and let out a piercing whistle of celebration that echoed through the arena, mingling with Davian's roar.

Othello wrapped his arms across Bjartur's snout as they laughed. Then Verena and Davian rushed to envelope them in tearful, laughter-filled hugs and congratulations.

"I hope you'll stay here with us, Othello."

He looked around, eyes sparkling in the firelight. "I think I might. You've really built something special here."

"It's no Dragon Palace."

"Who said I wanted a palace? But I *will* need a new lift."

One big enough for me too. I think it's time I explored the city below once again. A youthful shine glinted in Bjartur's eyes as he shook his wings and tapped his claws.

First thing tomorrow, I'll order the supplies. Maybe even convince them to give us a discount. Davian batted his eyes, and they laughed.

"If anyone could, it'd be you." Verena rolled her eyes with a grin.

As they made their way to the private living quarters of the volunteers and staff, Verena committed to the fresh idea brewing between her and Davian.

"I think if you're both up to the challenge, I have a special proposition for you."

Othello and Bjartur waited with wide eyes.

Verena cleared her throat. She wished Davian were speaking instead; he would find a way to say it more eloquently than her. He nudged her reassuringly. *Remember, I chose you for a reason too, and it wasn't your looks.*

She laughed, and the nervousness in her stomach dissipated. "I've always prided myself on being the most modern hatching ground with the most accepting regulations. But I was neglecting an entire demographic of creatures like yourselves without even knowing it. Now that I know better, I can't ignore it any longer. I want to open this hatching ground even further, extending the invitation to all Duvarharians with conditions which may keep them from their right to bond. What would you two say to managing a new division dedicated to serving that demographic of dragons and riders?"

The silence unnerved Verena. Then she saw tears in the newly bonded pair's eyes and realized they were discussing the proposition quietly, their thoughts and minds as seamlessly connected as Verena and Davian's.

When Othello turned back to her, she knew

the answer before he even spoke.

"Count us in."

AS VERENA CURLED UP by Davian's warm chest, a fur thrown over her body and her head nestled on the soft underbelly of his leg, she smiled up at the open, starry sky above her. The rock of the arena walls was still warm underneath her from the day's heat. By morning, it would cool, but Davian's body would keep her warm.

Perhaps with Othello around and a new crowd of riders and dragons coming in, you'll decide to socialize more.

Verena scoffed and fluffed up the fur, pulling it to her chin as she gazed into her dragon's eyes. "Doubtful." But she couldn't help but wonder if he was right. She'd spent the last thirty years of her life in the same daily routine of managing the hatching grounds. It'd been so long since anything had changed, she couldn't distinguish any of those years from each other. They all blurred together in one hazy memory.

Perhaps she'd started to believe nothing could

change for herself, that she'd found all life had to offer. But Othello and Bjartur had proved her wrong. No matter how old she became or what obstacles she faced, new chances and adventure could always be waiting just around the corner. Who knew what the next day would bring?

A nervous smile decorated her face as she looked to the stars once again. "I wonder what the Centaurs are reading in them tonight."

Davian turned one of his eyes to the skies, following her gaze. *They do seem brighter than usual.*

"Maybe they're celebrating Othello and Bjartur's bonding."

Davian rumbled in agreement then fell silent for a moment before he thought, *Or maybe they're celebrating how irresistibly beautiful we are.*

"Stars of all, be quiet, you egotistic maniac," she groaned. "I honestly don't know why I put up with you." But as she closed her eyes to welcome the sweetness of sleep, she knew exactly why. Because he was hers, and she was his. They'd chosen each other, and nothing would ever change that.

GLOSSARY

DUVARHARIAN

Fuse — A very large breed of buffalo-like pack animals

Fuju — Whiskey

Hanluurasa — The sky realm

Hanluu Lure Kusos — Sky Lake Tavern

Kijaqumok — Ancient Corrupt Magic

Kinuneb — Six Arms (a six-piece Duvarharian board game)

Klushuuv sub — Flirting trollop

Lurujmu fuju — Malt whiskey

Mumożelu — Fool

Nufa — Extremely vulgar Duvarharian expletive

Q.RJ.M (*Quźech raź jin mraha*) — After our Lord.

The age after the Great Lord's reign.

Rusadabe — Mountain goat native to Duvarharia

Sufax(ab) — Bastard(s)

Susahu — The realm of Darkness; Hell

Suźefrusum — Peaceful Forest (forest surrounding the Dragon Palace Valley)

Xeneluch ue — Dragon shit

SHÁZUK (RAVENWOOD CENTAURS)

Faykami — Scone-like pastry

Gauyuyáwa —Tree of our Rathers (ancestors); Center of Trans-Falls

Kodaazeñi — Warrior leaves (herb used to heal bruising)

Leño-zhego — Species of wildflower native to Ravenwood

Muluk — Drink made from steeping herbs, beans, or roots

Ñáwag-gazu — Species of intelligent mockingbird native to Ravenwood

Uwarñoe — High Medic

Woy-yulu kakezh — A non-sweet pastry

Zelauwgugey — Forest essence; Lyre of the Fauns

Zheborgiy — Witch's dream (a psychedelic fungus used to reduce pain)

Zuru fuñofufe —Damn this

SOCROLLEN

Socrolle — Southern country of Centaurs (not allied with Ventronovia)

Sichas — Capital city of Socrolle

Ema ar Gis — City of Power (Sichas)

Blarta — Second largest city in Socrolle

Esgren cuebre — A very light, rich, circular cake with a hole in the center

Dore — Citrus fruit native to Socrolle

BONUS CONTENT

Athena's Triple-Fruit Scones From the Dancing Tree Bakery

FAYKAMI

WITH DOLE GLAZE

Though some think them intimidating, scones are a rather easy pastry to make and are delightful plain or with glaze and a cup of tea or coffee.

Don't forget to make the glaze a couple days in advance

Preheat oven to 400°F

INGREDIENTS:

FOR THE PASTRIES:

3 cups flour

1/3 cup sugar

1 tablespoon baking powder

½ teaspoon baking soda

¼ teaspoon salt

6 teaspoons chilled butter

1/3 cup chopped dried apricots

1/3 cup chopped dried cranberries (craisins)

¾ cup low-fat buttermilk

Any fruit/flavorings/spices listed can be substituted with others

2 teaspoons grated orange rind

1 large egg

1 large egg white

FOR THE GLAZE:

1 1/4 cups sifted powdered sugar

1 1/2 tablespoons half and half or whole milk

Lemon juice and/or orange juice to taste (or vanilla and grated lemon/orange rind)

PASTRY INSTRUCTIONS:

Grease cookie sheet with lard, olive oil, or another non-stick substance.

Combine flour, sugar, baking powder, baking soda, and salt; cut in butter with a fork or pastry blender until resembles coarse meal. Stir in apricots and cranberries. In a separate bowl, combine buttermilk, orange rind, egg, and egg white; add to flour mixture, stirring just until moist.

Turn dough out onto a lightly floured surface; kneed lightly 4 times with floured hands. Roll dough into a rectangle roughly 12x6 inches. Cut dough into 8 (3x3-inch) squares. Cut each square into 2 triangles; place on greased baking sheet.

Bake at 400°F for 12 minutes or until golden. Makes about 16 scones.

Let cool on wire rack before topping with glaze.

GLAZE INSTRUCTIONS:

Sift the powdered sugar to remove clumps. Measure out 2 cups by spooning sugar into the cup and gently patting it level.

Add sugar to medium mixing bowl. Start adding the half and half or whole milk one tablespoon at a time. Wisk together for around two minutes or until smooth. Consistency should be thin enough to drizzle over the pastries, but thick enough to form a nice layer.

Then whisk in your choice flavorings (citrus juice or vanilla and grated citrus rinds)

GLAZING THE PASTRIES:

Once your pastries are completely cool, drizzle the glaze across them. If you have any extra grated rinds, you can sprinkle them on top of the glaze for added garnish. The glaze will dry and harden.

Brew some coffee or tea and enjoy!

If they don't sell out fast enough, they keep well wrapped in paper under a glass cover

Athena's Blueberry Lemon Bundt Cake from the Dancing Tree Bakery

ESGREN CUEBRE

WITH DOLE GLAZE

Simple but delightful, this bundt cake is large enough (and tasty enough!) to be paired with a cup of tea or coffee and shared with friends.

Pre-slicing and wrapping the cake saves time if the bakery is busy later

Preheat oven to 350°F

INGREDIENTS:

FOR THE CAKE:

1/3 cup butter, softened

4 ounces cream cheese, softened

2 cups sugar

3 large eggs, room temperature

1 large egg white, room temperature

1 tablespoon grated lemon zest

2 teaspoons vanilla extract

You can substitute any of the fruits or flavoring

2 cups fresh or frozen unsweetened blueberries

3 cups all-purpose flour, divided

1 teaspoon baking powder

1/2 teaspoon baking soda

1/2 teaspoon salt

1 cup lemon yogurt

FOR THE GLAZE:

1 1/4 cups confectioners' sugar

2 tablespoons lemon juice

PASTRY INSTRUCTIONS:

Grease and flour a ten-inch bundt pan. Cream the butter, cream cheese, and sugar in a large mixing bowl until blended. Add eggs and egg white one at a time, beating well after each is added. Beat in vanilla and lemon zest.

Lightly coat blueberries in 2 tablespoons flour. In a separate bowl, combine remaining flour with baking powder, baking soda, and salt. Alternate adding the dry ingredients and lemon yogurt to creamed mixture, beating after each is added just until combined. Fold in blueberry mixture.

Pour batter into the prepared pan. Bake at 350°F

for 55-60 minutes or until a toothpick or fork inserted into the center comes out clean. Leave in the pan to cool for 10 minutes before removing and transferring cake to a wire rack. Cool completely.

GLAZE INSTRUCTIONS:

Mix confectioners' sugar and lemon juice in a small bowl until smooth.

GLAZING THE CAKE:

Once the cake is completely cool, drizzle the glaze over it. You can take care to make sure it runs in even drips down the side of the cake for added aesthetic. If you have any extra grated rinds, you can sprinkle them on top of the glaze for garnish. The glaze will dry and harden.

If the cake is being eaten within the next few days (it most likely won't last even that long!), you can leave it covered on the counter.

Slice a piece, brew some coffee or tea, and enjoy!

Pairs nicely with a cup of hot lemongrass muluk with a hint of honey

Zheborgiy

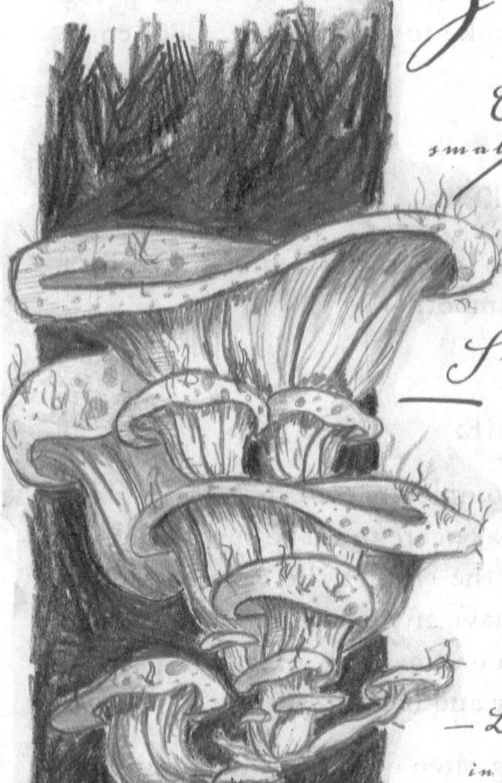

Cap (edible in small quantities raw)

Hairs (poisonous)

Stem (edible after processing)

Medicinal Uses

— Psycadelic
— Reducing Pain

Harvesting

— Large clusters grow high in trees. Can shoot down with arrows
— Usually found on the north side of tree trunks

Processing

— Dried & crushed in Muluk
— Smashed for postions or salves

Kodaazeñi

Blosoms (most potent)

Medicinal Uses

— Reducing Swelling & Bruising

Stem (can be used if absolutely needed)

Harvesting

— Hand pick with gloves or clean hands

— Harvest just before blooms are fully mature

Processing

— Do not injest until dilluted in alcohol

— Blosoms can be dried and mixed with oils and other herbs for a topical salve

Roots (can be used if needed but not recommended)

LETTER TO THE READERS

I WRITE THIS SMALL LETTER just after finishing editing my favorite story in this collection, "A Very Hungry Muse", and I am already wanting to dive back into Rasa and see what other stories and characters are waiting to be found and met.

Many years have passed since I first dreamt up Rasa as a wee young lass of twelve years. The world has since grown as I have, and over the years, I've met and visited hundreds of incredible characters and fascinating locations. But as I explored Rasa while writing The Shadows of Light series, I soon realized it was much too expansive to fit into just one series.

With dozens of unseen characters, locations, cultures, and backstories, I knew I would need some other way outside of The Shadows of Light to show Rasa's true depth. Thus, a short story collection was in order.

If I wasn't already in love with Rasa before writing this collection, I am absolutely smitten now.

I loved being able to explore existing characters' backstories like Aeron, Frawnden, and Jargon in "A Matchmaking Medic", and prelude to characters who have yet to debut in a main series such as Nescres, Athena, and Citana in "Dreaming of Freedom and Pastries". I also enjoyed being able to paint a picture of what Duvarharian dragon culture looked like during the Golden Years, such as in "Grounded Together", and what life would've been like for the Centaurs after the Sleeping, as in "Silence of Sleep in a Forest so Deep". And perhaps most exciting was being able to write "A Very Hungry Muse", which takes place in the Dragon Palace itself and whose characters I loved so much, I may decide to give them their own novel.

Rasa is real to me. It's not just a world in a book. It's a world of magic, dreams, potential. It's a world to get lost in, and to find some amount of home in for those who've felt out of place on Earth.

It's a world that's always just a page away.

Thank you for joining me in exploring Rasa, and I hope you have fallen in love with it as much as I have.

May the suns smile upon your presence.

—Effie Joe Stock

ACKNOWLEDGEMENTS

ODD AS IT MAY BE, I want to first thank the characters of this collection for showing up to tell me their beautiful stories and allowing me to be the honored scribes of their lives. I've never written anything so easy as this collection, and potentially never been so tenderly in love with anything I've written. None of it could've been possible if it weren't for the breath of life in each of these characters.

I also want to thank Nathaniel Luscombe for cheering me on during the creation of this collection, and whose comments after his initial reading of "A Very Hungry Muse" gave me the courage to continue. Thank you for dealing with my constant messages of "NATHANIEL!" when I'm desperate for you to respond.

Though I love baking, I don't do it often enough to have a large collection of my own pastry recipes (besides some cookies and scones), which is why I immediately ran to Andy for his delicious bundt cake recipe. I can't wait to have it again!

Thanks to my mother for giving me the idea of Frawnden and Aeron shooting through rings for the archery competition after Heather, my editor, shot down (pun intended) my first (very cliché) idea of having them split arrows.

Huge thanks to H. A. Pruitt for being an amazing editor and supporter. I always love everything you have to say about Rasa and the books in it, and I appreciate your brutal honesty more than you know. Special thanks for pointing out the glaring mathematical error in my family's scone recipe. I'll be sure to update that one in our collection!

Thank you to every follower who's supported me online, and of course, to YOU the reader who went the extra mile and not only read this collection but also this acknowledgment section. You make this all worthwhile and possible.

MORE BY
DRAGON BONE PUBLISHING

Bleached Reminders

Moon Soul

The Planets We Become

Turklet, Squeaky, and the Seven Chicken Chicks

The Shadows of Light Series:

Child of the Dragon Prophecy

Heir of Two Kingdoms

ANTHOLOGIES:

Aphotic Love

The Dragon Bone Journal, 2024 Issue

www.ingramcontent.com/pod-product-compliance
Lightning Source LLC
Chambersburg PA
CBHW010400310726
48979CB00017B/2793/J

* 9 7 8 1 9 6 2 3 3 7 0 4 5 *